LISTEN TO ME!

DEDICATION

To my mother, who I miss every day, you have always been my inspiration and my best friend. When I feel I can't do something, I hear your voice telling me I can. Thank you for giving me the tools in life to believe in myself.

1

Stepping off the bus, I cursed as my boot sunk into the cold, muddy puddle. I would have to make the twenty-minute walk to the garage with a frozen, ice-cold foot. My car was in for a broken wing mirror. Some idiot side swiped me and drove off leaving me shaken on the side of the road. I didn't stand a chance finding him. All this leading to yet another expense I didn't need this time of year. The freezing wind sliced through my gloves, and I wrapped my thick jacket around me trying to stay warm. I hated December and its' dark nights and miserable weather.

"Prick," I hissed, blaming the hit and run driver for the coldness seeping through my tights. The little town of Havant was busy with last-minute shoppers buying gifts and heading home. Lowering my head against the cold, I turned up my music tuning out the town noise.

Nearing the bridge that took me over the train line and onto Third Avenue, my heart started hammering. I hated walking this bridge at night. It always gave me an odd feeling. Even though nothing ever happened, I would laugh at myself every time I reached the end.

I skipped to the next track and let 'Encore' by Catfish and the Bottlemen fill my ears. The band was a favorite of mine. Realizing I was halfway over the bridge, a chill ran up my spine. A dark figure loomed in the distance...very still at first...taunting my sixth sense. Every nerve in my body screamed for me to turn and run. Frozen, unable to move, it turned like a doll spinning in a music box with its limbs unnaturally bent. I pulled my earphones out of my ears hearing a low, rattling sound that began to grow louder.

"*Stop!*" The warning was raspy, like sandpaper and I didn't need to be told twice. I charged back the way I had come, headed towards the train station just down the road, and jumped into a waiting taxi. Rattled and panting for breath, I abandoned the walk and vowed to never go that way again.

"You OK, love?" the taxi driver asked as I fell into the back seat a shaking mess.

"Yeah, bad day." I couldn't exactly tell him I might have seen a ghost. I gave him my address in Denvilles, and he chatted on about the weather and Brexit. A subject I'd given up talking about a long time ago.

The lights were on as I approached home. It was a comforting sight that calmed my nerves. Paying the cab driver, I ran through the front door and was relieved to feel the warmth. "Bloody Hell, what's up with you?" Justin, my husband, asked looking up from the TV as I slammed the door. I debated if telling him the truth was a good idea, but I needed to talk it out to so I could settle my mind. I recounted the whole story while he sat staring at me blankly. A reaction I expected.

"Really? Good one," he laughed and returned to the TV.

"Thanks for the support...I'm fine, by the way. Your concern is touching," I

3

snapped and stomped upstairs in search of a hot, relaxing shower.

Finished with the shower, I dressed in my warm night wear, wrapped myself up in a blanket and curled up on the bed to sulk. A few minutes later, the door opened, and Justin stood with an apologetic look and a large glass of wine.

"Peace offering?" he said with a puppy dog look.

"Is it my favorite?" I asked, still sulking. He nodded slightly, a smile curving the corners of his mouth.

"I'm sorry. Whatever you thought you saw, has scared you and I should've been more sympathetic." He sat on the bed next to me and rubbed my back. I took the wine and smiled at him.

"I know you think all that stuff is bullshit, but I swear something weird was on that bridge."

He kissed my forehead and tucked the blanket around my legs, "You're safe now. Tomorrow is an emotional day for you, and you know it always messes with you head."

Sighing, I knew he was right and felt utterly stupid. I was always a bag of nerves around this time of year.

"Are you all set for tomorrow?" Justin asked.

"No, I never am."

"I walked past that house this morning...it's still as creepy as ever. Do you remember? ...back in the day?" I wanted to change the subject, and this was all I could think of.

Justin laughed, throwing back his head, "How could I forget! We had so much fun back then." His smile dropped, and we both felt the pang in our chests at the childhood memory.

There was an old house set back along the Billy line, built in 1802 and belonged to the Cavangh family. Its last remaining occupant had reportedly died back in 1997. Abandoned and chained shut, it had been that way for the past twenty years. Rumor had it the house was haunted by Dougie Cavangh. Back in the day, our gang had spent many a night searching that house for his ghost. I swear I saw him once floating at the top of the stairs, but I don't think my friends had believed me. My best friend, Sophia had listened to my crazed story and didn't laugh at me, but we never mentioned it again. That was the last time I set foot in that house.

My heart lurched at the memory of Sophia. Her sweet photo sat on my bedside table. I had taken it on her sixteenth birthday, just before the party started to jump. It was the last photo I had taken; the last party she'd ever attended. The past ten years had passed with endless questions, but no answers. Sophia had vanished that night without a trace. I still wake up in the middle of the night in a cold sweat with a dread in my stomach. I've never been able to say the words, the ones on everyone's lips...

Sophia is dead.

Since then, everyone has moved on with their lives, apart from her parents. I still visit them regularly and we continue to hope she will walk through the front door one day. I know deep down that won't happen, but I'm not ready to give up on her...not yet. Sophia had been the best friend anyone could have funny, kind and loyal. I sometimes used to get irritated by her kindness. People took advantage and she'd let them. She always saw the good in everyone, even when they hurt her. I, on the other hand, am less forgiving. It seems even more so these days. My pain is still strong learning to live without her, but the worst is the not knowing. Did she run away, or did someone hurt her? Then on comes the guilt. I'm her best friend and I'm just carrying on with my life. She wasn't at my wedding, and she should've been. She should've been my Matron of Honor.

The search for her was intense but there was no evidence, no sightings, no witnesses, not even a clue on her computer or phone. Sophia had just vanished without a trace. It was as if she'd never existed.

This coming week is always so tough. Mentally and emotionally, it's still almost too hard to bare.

Her parents host an anniversary gathering yearly on her birthday, Dec 5th.

Unfortunately, it also commemorates the day she disappeared.

"What happened?" I whispered and ran my finger over her face. Tears ran down my cheeks as I gazed at her photo, missing her so much.

Justin placed his finger over mine, "One day we'll find the truth."

Justin had been at school with us and was a part of our gang. He had moved away for a few years once we'd left school but returned five years ago. We'd met at a club one Saturday night and I immediately noticed how 'grown up' he had become. Now, here we were six months into our marriage and soul mates. Funny how things work out in life. I'd never thought of him like that at school.

"I promise you one day we will have closure. Now get some rest." He flicked on our bedroom TV and left me to catch up on Game of Thrones...I had discovered it later than the rest of the world and was still binge-watching Season four. Now that I was still, I noticed my aching feet. Between standing on my feet all day at the clothing store, walking everywhere while the car was in the shop, and running a half marathon to get away from the bridge phantom, I was exhausted. I didn't have the strength to fight my eyes closing and I let sleep take over

2

I couldn't breathe.

I couldn't see.

I gagged as the water filled my mouth.

The surrounding sound took a while to register. Running water and the pain in my head blurred my vision. Forcing my eyes to peer open, I focused on the dark outline of a person, but I couldn't tell if it was a man or women. I could hear muttering. It was a low sound that I could only grasp a few words from.

"Look what you made me do. Little Bitch ..."

I tried to scream, but no sound would come. My sight faded to black with the memory of the sound of the water falling on me and I knew I was dying. As hard as I tried, I couldn't get out of the water. The longer I was pushed under and held firmly down, the less strength I had to fight back. I was suffocating.

I woke just as I hit the floor. Sweat poured from me, and Justin sprung over the bed. "Jesus, what the fuck!" He picked me up and held me until I had calmed down. I cried against his chest and his arms tightened, comforting me until the tears stopped and the panic had subsided.

"It was just a nightmare. You're safe." He kissed my forehead. "Same one?" He asked.

"Yeah." I had the same dream repeatedly around this time of year. My doctor claims it's due to stress and pain the anniversary caused me. To help me cope, he prescribed anti-depressants about three years ago after a terrible few months. Delayed shock or something like that. They helped, but it didn't stop the dreams from coming several times a year.   "Go back to sleep." Justin suggested. I glanced at the clock. It was six-thirty, and I knew I wouldn't sleep now. I stumbled to the kitchen on shaky legs and made a strong coffee, preparing for the day.

3

I waited in my car for a few minutes, taking a few breaths and a bit of time to compose myself. I hated this day but loved it at the same time. I would never miss this anniversary. Even though I wanted to curl up under my duvet and hide until the day passed, I couldn't do that to her parents.

"Ready?" Justin asked taking my hand in his. I nodded, "I guess."

People had arrived, but I waited until I saw the blue BMW pull up behind me. I got out and my dad pulled me in for one of his hugs. Nothing feels safer than a hug from your dad.

"I've got you," he assured me. "Ten years...I can't believe it." He sounded choked up, his voice wavering. "Such a lovely girl."

"Where's mum?" I asked, noticing her absence. My dad frowned and sighed heavily.

"She's not coming. We aren't talking, again. She felt it wasn't appropriate for us both to be here if we are having a domestic."

"What is going on with you two?" I knew things hadn't been great lately. I feared they were slowly drifting apart but I couldn't get a straight answer out of them as to what was wrong.

"Don't worry about that, we will be just fine. If anyone asks, she's ill. OK?"

I nodded reluctantly, but agreed it was the best thing. My parents' marital problems were not the concern of Sophia's family. Dad greeted my husband with a firm handshake, and they did the usual small talk. They got on...which was a bonus. Dad had liked no one I'd dated until Justin. Their love of football and cricket had bonded them, plus both being avid Portsmouth FC Fans had sealed the deal.

As we approached the front door, I sucked in my breath and rang the doorbell. Yvonne, Sophia's mum, answered giving me a slight grin.

"Kim, so lovely to see you." I could see the tears, although she held them back. I hugged her tightly, and she kissed my cheek.

She ushered us through, and I looked around at the memories staring back at me. They had decorated the house with photos and banners saying happy birthday, and more food than needed. Yvonne always busied herself playing the host. It was the only way she'd get through the day.

"You've always been her most loyal friend. I'm so glad you have never forgotten her." She tucked my hair behind my ears, the longing look in her eyes; a mother with so much love and no child to give it to. My heart broke for her.

"I never will forget. I miss her every second of every day."

She hugged Justin and thanked him for his loyalty before sucking in her breath and straightening up; her host face was back.

"I'd better get more drinks." She hurried off to the kitchen before emotions overcame her.

My dad appeared at my side, handing over a glass of Prosecco. I stared into the pale, shimmering liquid and wondered if Sophia would've been a fan of this drink or more of a spirit girl. We'd never gotten that far. The odd night of ciders or cans of beer that our friend Lewis would steal from his dad was our drink of choice back then. We'd hang out hiding in the park or, if we felt brave, in the Cavangh house. A chill ran through me at the thought of that place. Lately, those odd feelings had been more frequent.

"Kim!" The shout made me jump, but I knew that voice. I turned with a smile and outstretched my arms. Lewis bounded towards me, all six feet of him, and lifted me up. It had been a year to the day since I had seen him on Sophia's last anniversary.

Lewis lived in Covent Garden, his ideal place to live. He's an amazing actor and currently involved in the musical, Fame. It was a career he was born to follow; always singing, dancing, and working his way up to much bigger things. He'd done many shows in the west end, a few small parts in TV, but his ultimate dream was to have a leading role in a movie. He'd get there one day; I had no doubt of that. He was never short of confidence, nor would he let anyone tell him he couldn't do things. He'd always prove you wrong. Lewis has been a good friend, and we both shared the loss of Sophia. I don't think he'd ever gotten over it, especially since they had been a couple before she went missing. He'd liked her since junior school. It wasn't until they started secondary school, they'd become more than that.

They had been a sweet couple. He adored her then and still did now. None of his relationships over the years had lasted. I think it's because the unanswered fate of Sophia plagued him. He told me once he felt guilty and, in some ways, betraying her. He never got to say goodbye, or in his words 'protect her.' I don't think he'll ever be happy until we know what happened that day and finally put her to rest. He put on a front most of the time, but when it was just the two of us, he'd allow himself to be honest. His hug lingered, squeezing me tight. "Put me down, you daft sod. I can't breathe." He let me go seeing Justin behind me. 'Justin, mate, good to see you too'.

"It's good to see you, Lewis. How are things?'" he responded, grabbing a beer from the table.

Lewis told us about the show, and how he'd dated again for a while. It was the usual story of things being great at first, but it just didn't work out. His sister had gotten married the previous month to a man Lewis couldn't stand. Although he never told me why he didn't like him, he just didn't.

We stood talking and reminiscing and the hours flew by. It was nice to catch up. Remembering the stories and adventures of our teenage years seemed easier to talk about this time. I smiled when Sophia came into the story, but deep down, it still stung.

Mid conversation, the music started and instantly I grabbed for Lewis's hand. It shook in my grip as Christina Perri's, 'A Thousand Years' filled the room. It was their song. Sophia would sing it constantly back then while Lewis would roll his eyes at her attempt to sing. It was during our

Twilight obsession. The song meant something different to us both, and before we knew of it, we both sobbed in each other's arms. Every person in that house stood still, held hands or wiped tears from their eyes, but no words were muttered. Maybe, we needed it, to let it out fully, and I was grateful her mother had chosen that song. If Yvonne had found the strength to listen to such a specific thing associated to Sophia, maybe, just maybe, we were moving on.

I needed a tissue to dry my eyes and wipe my nose, so I quickly padded to their downstairs bathroom. It was only once I'd entered the hall, I heard the hysterical crying. It came from upstairs, and I immediately knew it was Yvonne.

Taking the stairs two at a time, I raced to Sophia's room. Yvonne was on her knees, screaming into Sophia's favorite pillow, a fluffy pink heart Lewis had given to her for Valentine's Day.

"Who did that?" she cried, her sobbing wrenching her chest. I fell beside her, pulling her against me trying to comfort her agony.   "I wish we knew; I

18

wish we knew where she was to," I said holding her closely. Yvonne shook her head frantically, and her grief-stricken eyes bored into mine.

"Did you, do it?" She snarled.

"What?! I wouldn't hurt her. Yvonne?" My heart burst with pain, but I could hardly believe what I was hearing. Was she accusing me?

Looking up at me, the sadness that overcame Yvonne's face was gut-wrenching. "I know you wouldn't, but who put that song on? Who did that? How could they?"

"I thought you had?" I answered with confusion.

"No! Why would I? I can't bear it; it breaks my heart too much!"

Quickly understanding it was the song that had caused her to lose composure, I let out a small breath. She hadn't picked that song.

"She would play it over and over and sing it constantly. It's a beautiful song but I can't hear it. Ever! It kills me too much." Yvonne sobbed into the pillow.

Rage pulsed through me. Everyone knew how much that song upset her parents and those close to her. I couldn't believe some insensitive idiot had played it anyway. I hugged Yvonne and reassured her I would be back to check in.

I stormed down the stairs, fury building so much that by the time I had reached the bottom I couldn't hold back.

"Who put that song on? Who?" I screamed as I scanned the room, waiting for the guilty party to move. Every conversation stopped, drinks and plates held statue still as blank but concerned faces stared at me.

"Yvonne didn't! Everyone knows how she feels about it! So, who!?" I waited, my patience almost at an end. Justin moved forward to embrace me and calm me down. It didn't work.

"She is upstairs in a terrible state!" I couldn't stop the onslaught of angered words that escaped my mouth. "Which one of you did it!?"

Everyone denied it, all assuring me they hadn't. Lewis looked devastated. He said nothing at first until he stood and joined me.

"All I can say is, whoever it was, you are one insensitive prick. That was our song, more hers, but it means so much to me too. I'd happily hear it if her parents agreed, but not if it causes them pain." His voice was calm, but the undertone was angry.

Turning, he left the house and sat in the back garden on a bench specifically placed in memory of Sophia. Her favorite place to sit and read. I watched him for a minute or two, giving him a little space. He was still at first, but then he suddenly jumped from the bench and spun around as if looking for something.

I went to him and the shock on his face stopped me in my tracks. "Lewis, what's wrong?"

He shook his head and rubbed his face with his hands. "I'm OK, that song has just thrown me. I'm hearing things."

He didn't seem to want to continue the conversation, so I let it go. The song had shaken everyone up.

We sat for a few minutes before heading back inside. More people had arrived, and Yvonne had returned to her guests with a forced smile. The new arrivals were familiar faces and ones I was happy to see. Adam Price stood awkwardly in the kitchen looking a bit lost. Yvonne handed him a beer, and they chatted quietly. Adam smiled as I approached.

"Oh my God, I'm so pleased you're here." I smiled, excited to see him as he wrapped me in a hug.

"I had to come this time. I've felt terrible the last few years." Adam hadn't attended the previous four years; working in Japan made it difficult. He was an English teacher, and it wasn't easy to take time off.

"Its fine, we all understand. Sophia would be so proud of you. She always said you were a great teacher."

Adam nodded and took a sip of his beer. "I was always helping her with her homework." Sophia hated homework and Adam was the cleverest of the gang. Academically, it wasn't a surprise he would go into teaching because he had a gift. He would always stay patient, even though he found most things easy. He accepted the fact the rest of us weren't as clever, never making others feel belittled or stupid. I guess you could call him the nerd of the group, but we didn't see him that way. Adam was the sweetest guy and had always been there as a good friend. I was so happy he'd turned up.

"You helped her so much. I don't think she would've done so well without you."

He shrugged. "I didn't mind, and she was a friend." He frowned as talking about her was still hard for him too. "I can't believe it's been ten years. Still nothing?" he asked.

I shook my head, "Nope." I sighed as the actual thought exhausted me.

Lewis entered the kitchen and man-hugged his old friend. "Adam! Mate!"

I left them to catch up and headed back to the living room where Yvonne was asking about the song. Oddly, nobody seemed to look remotely guilty, in fact, they were all just as confused.

"Maybe, it was just a coincidence. *Spotify* can just start playing songs at random." I suggested.

Keith, Sophia's dad, moved to put his arm around his wife. He had said little, never did at these gatherings. He endured the get together more for Yvonne. If Keith were honest, he'd be happier not doing it. He preferred to remember his daughter in private. I could see him looking at his watch regularly and hoping the day would be over soon. The day his daughter was born and the day she had been taken from them.

For the first time today, Keith spoke, "I agree, nobody would be so insensitive. I'm sure it's what Kim said. Don't upset yourself, love." Keith softly said, letting his arm slide down to hold his wife's hand. She took it and squeezed it tightly.

"I feel so stupid now." Yvonne accepted her husband's answer and apologized for her outburst. There wasn't anyone there who would hold it against the grieving mother.

Further arrivals made the day complete. The final few of our old school gang had made the trip; Chloe Boston, Matt Hines and Darren Hewitt turned up together as a surprise.

"Why didn't you tell me you were coming?" I screamed as I ran to Chloe.

"We wanted to surprise you. Plus, I didn't know for sure until late last night." Chloe remarked.

She was as stunning as she'd always been. Now a fully qualified beautician and working in London for a very expensive beauty salon. Darren had been her boyfriend in school, but they were only friends now. Although, if he had his way, they'd still be together. I never understood why they broke up. Chloe had just said 'Oh, I just don't think of him like a boyfriend anymore. I love him, but I'm not in love. Do you know what I mean?' He'd seemed cut up about it. That had been a week before Sophia had disappeared. They had stayed friends because finding Sophia had been more important.

Chloe was engaged to a guy named Chris who was in LA producing an album with a new band. I'd forgotten their name already. They suited each other; both beautiful and liked the finer things in life. Chloe rooted inside her Gucci leather bag. A bag I know cost near to two thousand pounds. Another gift from the wonderful Chris.

Darren worked as a waiter for a restaurant in Gunwharf Quays while he studied for his law degree. I could see the envy on his face when Chloe talked about 'her Chris.' She wasn't a bad person, in fact she was very sweet, but she had expensive taste. I noticed Matt stood back…a little less enthusiastic.

"Matt, good to see you." I said, he smiled and nodded.

"Where's the booze?" he asked, his tone was tense. I led him to the kitchen.

"What's wrong?" I asked, handing him a beer. He sighed and leaned against the kitchen side.

"Her." he snapped.

"Chloe?"

"Yeah, she just gets on my nerves sometimes. Chris this, Chris that, look what he's given me. Look how much this cost...Fuck off." Matt had always been less fond of Chloe. They just clashed.

"You know she means no harm."

He shrugged his shoulders, "I know, but today isn't a time to go acting a knob. Nobody gives a fuck about her fucking boyfriend. She hasn't shut up about him all the way here." He closed his eyes tightly and shook himself. "Sorry, that was harsh. I needed to rant for a second. And Darren needs to stop looking at her with puppy dog eyes. It's pathetic."

Matt had never handled this well. He came out of duty, never wanting to let Sophia down. His anger projected at others, usually Chloe.

"Feel better now you've got that off your chest?"

"Yes, now I'll shut up." We chatted for a while longer before we returned to the others. Matt was much calmer and settled into the conversation. Justin wrapped his arm around my shoulders as we laughed at old memories. Sophia's family filled the house. Her brothers, her aunts, uncles, cousins, and her grandparents, and many family friends. The hours passed and as guests began to leave, I headed for the bathroom and heard whispers...angry whispers coming from Sophia's room. Before I reached the top of the stairs, Chloe came rushing out, tears soaked her cheeks. The door swung inwards, and Sophia's uncle stood inside looking concerned. I shouted after Chloe as she hurried down the stairs.

"I can't do this, it just hurts too much." she sobbed and disappeared through the house. I entered Sophia's room.

"What's wrong with Chloe?"

'" Same as the rest of us, still devastated. I found her in here crying. I tried to talk to her, but she wasn't up for it. I guess this room takes you back." Gary Mason was Keith's older brother, he was fifty-nine and had worked tirelessly over the years trying to find Sophia and it was taking its toll.

"I guess we've all got to deal with it in our own way."

Gary looked up, and the sadness in his face was hard to see.

"Yvonne is about to do the usual speech, we better go." he stood and headed back down. I quickly used the bathroom and hurried back too. Yvonne was addressing the guests, thanking them for coming as she talked about Sophia.

"Never forget her," she made us all promise, again. Then she shocked us all.

"I can't thank you all for the support over the years, but I must face the truth. My daughter isn't coming home. I can't keep expecting you all to drop everything and be here on her birthday. This is the last gathering I will be holding. I won't stop hoping, or loving her, but I need to stop torturing myself and all who loved her."

Sobs broke her tough stance and Keith supported his wife. He took over, "We will always celebrate the day she was born, and if you still want to be here, please come, but we no longer expect it."

It stunned me. I sure as hell didn't see that coming and I wasn't sure how I felt about it

4

I watched my dad drive away...a little of me worried for him. I didn't know what it was, but he wasn't himself; neither was my mother. I wasn't a child, but the thought of them divorcing made my heart wrench. He hadn't said it, but it was clear the marriage was at a breaking point. The evidence was there when I visited a few weeks back. Mum denied they were sleeping in separate rooms, but the fact all of Dad's stuff was in the spare room confirmed her lie.

No longer in my view, Dad's taillights disappeared. I continued to stare out my car window, my hands gripping the steering wheel. Yvonne's speech had hit me harder than I expected, and I could feel the overwhelming grief creeping up on me. My eyes stung as tears blurred my vision. I hadn't had a good hard cry for Sophia in a long time.

I started the engine and prepared to drive away when something in the distance made me stop. What the hell was that? I wiped my eyes and squinted trying to make out what was in the road. It was moving…almost staggering. Darkness made it hard to see clearly, but I was sure it was a person. Their head was down, and they moved unsteadily, hunched over so their face was hidden.

Thick fog wrapped around my car. The figure was inches from my bumper. Light flickered all around it as if candles burned behind smoke. As if in a trance, I couldn't move my eyes from the figure. It slowly lifted its' head. The scream caught in my throat, my body stiffened, and my eyes wouldn't move from her face. Sophia's face. Her hands jerked forward, and she crawled upwards towards the windshield…she was crying so softly.

"You won't believe me, please believe me. You need to listen, please listen…"

Sophia would have been twenty-six today, but this Sophia was still sixteen. She was blue and purple, and her eyes rolled to the back of her head. Her skin leathery and dry, stretched tight over her sunken face, and her teeth black. Her hair was dirty and matted. She scratched at the window.

"You lied. Why did you do this to me, I'll make you pay, I will."

I fought back my fear, this was my best friend. I snapped off my seatbelt and got out of the car. Stopping to look, my knees crumpled as I stared at the empty car bonnet.

"Sophia!"

Frantically I searched around the car but there was nothing, nobody at all, just me. The wind picked up and leaves whirled around me; it was loud and kept getting louder. The sound turned from wind to screams deep inside my head. It was like the noise trapped me. My hands gripped my ears. I could see her, hand outstretched and begging for help. She was in a dark space; her clothes were wet, and she was gasping between screams.

"Kim!"

My eyes popped opened, and I was back by my car gripping the bumper fiercely. My breathing erratic. Yvonne had seen me from her window and rushed out to check on me.

"Are you OK?" she asked as she pulled me up to my feet.

"I don't feel very well," I said leaning against her. "I need to lie down." She helped me back inside just as I blacked out.

It was dark when I woke later that night. They had tucked me under a duvet on the sofa. It was three-thirty in the morning, and all was silent in the house. It reminded me of sleepovers as kids. The house was still the same, and its' warmth hadn't changed. I stared up at the ceiling. The room above was Sophia's. Memories washed over me thinking about our younger days. We'd sit and chat about boys and clothes, the latest gossip at school with no cares in the world. I missed those days...they seemed so long ago. It made me smile for a few seconds.

A sound broke through my reminiscing and made me sit straight up. Footsteps above me, loud and deliberate. I listened. Maybe Yvonne was in Sophia's room. I heard faint crying, low, but I knew it was her mother. Throwing off the duvet, I headed upstairs to comfort her. It was chilly at the top of the stairs and Sophia's room was empty. I shivered at how cold it was. Had Yvonne already left the room? Did I miss her by seconds? No, I would have heard her walking back to her room... the floorboards were old and creaked all the time. I stood in the bedroom and waited; the minutes ticked by, and I cursed myself. I was hearing things. Maybe it was just the usual noises houses make in the dead of night. I turned to head back downstairs, my hand on the doorknob.

"Don't go." The voice was eerily soft. Goosebumps spread over my body as I slowly turned towards the sound. She stood with her back to me, looking out of the bedroom window. Tears pricked at my eyes.

"Sophia" I said, my shaking hand stretched out as I eased forward.

"Why?"' she whispered back.

"Sophia tells me what happened, please."

Her body began to shake violently, a rattling sound vibrated from her. Her head turned unnaturally.

"Can't...tell...you..."

"Why? Why can't you tell me!?"

"You won't believe me, and you'll hate me."

Her face twisted with pain and as quickly as she appeared, she melted away and was gone, the window empty now.

"Sophia come back. I'd never hate you, let me help. Just tell me and I'll find you. Please come back," I begged.

A light flicked on in the hallway and this time I heard footsteps. Yvonne entered the room with a concerned look but was calm.

"Are you OK, Kim?"

I shook my head and burst into tears, sinking to my knees. Soft arms embraced me, and she whispered in my ear, "It's OK, Kim. I know what happened, she scared me to the first time she visited me."

I looked up at her, tears streaming down my face, my eyes wide. "You...you've seen her?"

She nodded and smiled. "Only recently. I thought I was losing my mind, but now that I know you've seen her, I know I'm not going crazy."

35

Yvonne pulled me up and sat me down on Sophia's bed. "I know she's dead now. I just need to know the truth. I need to know what happened and I need to put my baby to rest, like she deserves."

Sadness showed on her face as she left the room leaving me alone. A thought struck me. Did someone we know have something to do with Sophia's death? I felt dread in my stomach as Sophia's words rang in my head.

"You won't believe me, and you'll hate me."

5

I don't know how I ended up outside the Cavangh house. One minute I was walking home from the gym, and the next I was stood outside the shabby-looking house. Walking alongside the house and into the back garden, I saw the door that used to be the way in...our way inside back when we were kids. Batting away cobwebs, I opened the door and dirt cascaded on my head.

Nothing had changed. The same wallpaper falling away from the mold covered walls and the smell of must overtook my nostrils. At the end of the hall was the spacious lounge. At one time, it was probably homey and warm; now it stood cold, empty and lifeless. A green armchair sat in the middle of the room, the color faded and dirty. It was as if time stood still. I took a few steps to run my hand along the top of the old chair: the material rough under my hand. I took a deep breath and scanned the room.

Cold fingers gripped my hand tightly. I tugged at the fingers that pinned mine.

They were blue, and the skin was decaying. I was screaming but I couldn't get loose.

"You won't believe me."

I stopped struggling, my gaze landed on the arm. The pink watch, a present I had given Sophia on her sixteenth birthday, was buckled tightly to the bony wrist.

"No." The force pulled me over the chair, and I looked into my dead friend's eyes. "I'm not a bad girl... I'm not ..." My hand was released and I stumbled backwards.

Staggering out of the room, I stopped in the hall to catch my breath. A sound made me freeze. Footsteps walked above me, too loud and solid for a ghost. Someone was in the house. The footsteps were heading down the stairs. Fear pulsed through my body and I ran!

I didn't stop running until I was back home. I locked my front door behind me and collapsed into a heap on the floor. I cried until my throat hurt and I was exhausted.

Justin wasn't home, and he was all I needed. His calls went unanswered, so I took a hot shower and curled up on the sofa to wait for him.

I didn't move until I heard his key in the lock. He stumbled through the door, a bag of chips in his hand.

"Justin, where the hell have you been?!" I yelled. He looked at me, swayed a little and put a chip in his mouth and mumbled, "the pub." He staggered to the sofa and collapsed onto it.

"Sorry, only went for one after work but you know what the lads are like." I could smell the beer on his breath.

"A phone call would have been nice." I snapped.

"Sorry..." he mumbled and shoved more chips in his mouth. He held the bag towards me, but I pushed them away. I couldn't eat, not after earlier events.

"I've seen Sophia."

Justin stopped chewing and stared at me, struggling to keep his head swaying due to his current state.

"You've seen who?"

"Sophia."

His eyes widened, "They've found her?"

"No, but I've seen her ghost."

Justin put the bag of chips on the table and pulled me down to him. "Did you have another bad dream?"

I pulled away and looked him straight in the eyes. "No, it wasn't a dream. I know she's dead, because I have seen her ghost, more than once."

The silence from Justin made me look up at him; his mouth hung open.

"I know it sounds insane, but I'm telling the truth." Justin took my hand and nodded. "I think these visions or nightmares will never go away; not until you get some answers."

My heart dropped at his calm explanation. He wasn't mocking me but the pity in his eyes felt worse. I was too drained to argue my point, so I said nothing.

I headed to the kitchen and poured a large glass of wine, strolled back to the sofa and settled next to Justin sipping my wine. Feeling his gaze on me, I know he picked up on my pissed off vibe.

"I've pissed you off, I can tell."

"Nope." I said as calmly as possible; the tense tone of my voice gave me away.

"I think you need to go back to Louise."

I felt the rage erupt from the pit of my stomach. The mention of my old therapist made me lose my composure.

"I don't need a therapist…my best friend was murdered, and I need to find out what happened. No fucking therapist can help with that!" I snapped.

"Kim, this needs to stop. Every year the same thing happens. Dreams and panic attacks! Enough is enough. Sophia's gone. You need …"

"I need to what?" I slammed the wine glass down on the table. "Move on? Forget about her?" My voice rising at each word, and tears streaming down my face. My husband, the one person I should be able to trust had betrayed me; or at least that's how it felt in that moment.

"That's not what I meant. All I'm saying is… the stress isn't good for you. I want this to be over just as much as you do…to put her to rest and have closure. I just hate seeing you hurting."

I knew his words were the truth, but I couldn't help feeling angry towards him. I couldn't punish the person responsible. Justin was just in the firing line.

"I'm going to bed, and tomorrow I'll pretend Sophia never existed."

I stormed from the room. Anger pulsed through me mixed with guilt at my behavior. The lights were off upstairs, making me reach for the light switch. Cold fingers stopped me. A grip so hard I thought my hand would break. Breath like ice briefly fanned my hair and I heard muffled whispers fill my bedroom.

"Don't forget me…"

The room warmed, and the light flickered on. My hand stayed frozen in the same position and I stared at the handprint left behind.

"I don't know what to do," I sobbed. Justin had followed me. I knew he thought I was losing my mind. I saw it in the look in his eyes: concern, pity, but mostly fear.

"You need help..." he said and disappeared back down the stairs. My heart broke, but I didn't follow him. I needed time to myself to think about what was happening. This time differed from the previous years. I wasn't depressed. Something bigger was happening, and I needed to see it through to the end.

6

It was the cold breeze that woke me later that night. I shivered and felt around for my duvet to cover up. I couldn't find it. I waited for my vision to adjust to the dark. My duvet was missing.

Justin snored lightly next to me unaffected by the drop in temperature. I searched the floor but there was nothing. As I looked up, my duvet hovered in the doorway. I froze. It was wrapped around something…a figure. It shook underneath it. I couldn't see a face through the darkness, but I knew it was staring at me.

"It's… so… cold.'" The voice sounded strained, an echo to it. It was full of sadness. *"Wake up. Go back, Kim, Go back."*

The duvet lost its shape and fell to the floor. I don't know how long I stared at my bedroom doorway, but when I finally moved, I grabbed my duvet and curled up underneath it.

Bile rose in my throat at the thought that I knew who had killed Sophia. Didn't I? I must know them. I couldn't sleep now. I stayed awake with worried thoughts going around my mind. I couldn't comprehend the truth of how Sophia had died. It scared me to find out, but I had no choice.

I was staring at the ceiling when a shuffling noise made me jump. It was close, my side of the bed close. I forced myself to look and I was paralyzed with fear.

Sophia stood by my bedside. Her skin was decaying and flaking off, her eyes shimmered with tears.

"I miss you," Sophia whispered. *"Help me."*

"Help me," then she decayed rapidly, fell into pieces and vanished. I screamed hysterically causing Justin to jump up; expecting an intruder.

"What the fuck?!" His hands on his head, looking at me with disbelief, "I thought you were being attacked. These dreams are getting worse."

I was hyperventilating, and Justin reminded me to use the techniques we'd learned over the years. Counting helped me focus and control my breathing, it was the only thing that worked during a panic attack.

"It wasn't a fucking dream!" I yelled, shoving his hand away as he tried to pull me towards him.

"Sophia needs my help," I loved this man, but his refusal to listen to me would mean I would have to risk it. He'd see eventually that I wasn't having a breakdown; I never was. All this time my friend had been trying to reach me. I hadn't listened before, but I was wide awake now.

"Kim."

"No, Justin! I don't want to hear it. I know how this looks; I know you think I'm ill. Trust me, this is real. Sophia's ghost is real."

I felt a weight lift from me, and I spun in a circle. "I hear you Sophia. I'm sorry, but I am listening now."

Justin wrapped the duvet around me and guided me back to bed. His arms held me tight.

"OK, I believe you," he whispered. I knew he didn't, but it was his way of keeping me calm for now.

Tomorrow I would dig into what happened, with or without his help.

I spent the next few hours thinking about my next move until the sun came up. I showered and drank two very strong cups of coffee. I called my doctors and booked an appointment for later that day. I called into work and told them I was suffering with a stomach bug. That gave me the rest of the week off. The feeling of guilt only lasted a few minutes at my outright lie, but I couldn't say I was looking into my dead best friend's murder because she asked me to...could I?

I started by noting everything I could remember from that night.

They had held her party at the local rugby club. They had a room upstairs perfect for birthday parties. I had helped Sophia get ready at her house. I had been swimming in the morning, called Sophia at midday to gossip about the night ahead, before heading over around four. Nothing unusual. She was excited about the party and getting her new phone...the one she never got to use.

At five everyone began to arrive, family and friends. The DJ played all her favorite music and food was laid out down one side of the room. It was just a normal teenage birthday celebration. The only thing that happened that night was Chloe and Darren. I saw them arguing in the carpark around eight pm. Sophia ushered me back inside telling me to stay out of it. Later, they had seemed to have cleared the air. The two had just broken up and Sophia had claimed Darren had been hassling her to get back together. I had thought nothing of it. I tried to think of anything else from that night. We had eaten loads of food, sneaked around the back of the building around 9pm to drink cider. Matt and Darren had both started smoking; Darren had taken a few from his Dad's packet. They shared one cigarette before we rejoined the party. Around ten-thirty as the party was winding down, Sophia said she was going to the bathroom. That was the last time I ever saw her. We waited on the dance floor for her to come back and dance until the end. I never saw again her.

I went upstairs and pulled out the box I had kept of old childhood things. It had been ages since I had looked inside. I would collect things I felt were important and place them in this wooden box. Photos, birthday cards, and my old school shirt signed with messages from the last day of school filled the keepsake box. I cried as I looked through our old pictures, my heart bursting from the memories.

I'd forgotten how full the box was and took another look at the bottom of the box. I found something strange. A disposable camera hidden under some old schoolbooks. I frowned, confused at first, but then I remembered. Sophia's uncle had put one on each table at her party. He wanted a bit of retro; he hated all the new technology. They had been taken to the police ten years ago. I hadn't even used one so why was this one in my box?

I felt pin pricks all over my skin; I hadn't left the party with one so I couldn't have put one in my memory box. I stared at it as if it was an alien being before grabbing it, heading out my front door, jumping into my car, and taking off towards town. I needed to get them developed quickly. I dropped the camera into my local boots store before heading to my doctor's appointment. After a forty-five-minute wait, five minutes with my doctor, I had a sick-note signing me off work for two weeks. As bad as it was playing on my issues, I needed to do this.

As I drove home, I felt suddenly lighter...more determined. I had a purpose in my day now. It had always been there under the surface, and I would end this nightmare.

"Fuck!" I screamed, slamming on the breaks, as I looked in my rearview mirror. The face of Sophia was looking back at me. The seat was empty when I checked, but in the mirror she remained.

"Go back!" she screamed. *"Go back! I need you to know, but I know it will hurt..."* Sophia's tears wouldn't stop running down her cheeks.

I begged her to tell me. It didn't matter, I would believe her. Her head shook violently from side to side. *"No, I can't!"* she screamed before she vanished, and my back seat was empty

7

Yvonne carried a tray into the living room providing tea and biscuits for my unexpected visit. Although, she didn't seem overly surprised to see me.

"It's great you're here. I worried that after my little announcement, people would step away from us."

I held out my hand, grabbing hers. "I will always be here for you." I assured her. The smile she gave me was one of relief.

"You've always been like one of the family. It means a lot to hear that." She poured the tea, adding the milk and two sugars. She knew me well enough that she didn't need to ask.

"I need to ask you a few things...about that night. I don't want to drag up the past, but I need to find out what happened. I know there is something we've missed."

Yvonne closed her eyes, holding back tears I guessed. "Ok."' her voice was low, nervous.

"Did she say anything to you that day? Did anyone upset her?"

Yvonne shook her head. No, nothing. She was happy…excited." I told her about my memory box and the camera. "You think there might be something on there?"

I shrugged. "Honestly, I don't know. I didn't use one of those cameras and I didn't leave with one. I don't understand how one has appeared in my box."

Yvonne seemed to stiffen, her hands twitched. "That is very odd. When do you pick them up?"

I told her I would collect them the next day and let her know. We chatted for a bit longer, but the conversation led to nothing. Yvonne knew nothing more now as she did back then. The drive back home was lonely, I didn't even want to go there. Justin was due home soon and I would have to act all normal. I approached my house fifteen minutes later after being held at the train gates. They irritated me. Those gates were the bane of everyone's lives who lived close by. No bridge, so even people on foot couldn't get over.

It was dark already. It felt more like nine in the evening, not four-thirty in the afternoon. The lights were on and Justin's car was in the drive. Frowning, I shut off the car engine. Justine wasn't usually home before five.

"Justin?" I called as I entered. "Babe?"

I heard nothing at first, but then footsteps thumped towards me. His brood frame appeared from the dark staircase.

"Hey."

"Why are you home so early?" I asked, trying not to sound accusing.

"I felt bloody awful this afternoon. Might be coming down with something. I took time owed and came home."

I looked at his face, he looked pale.

"You don't look great." He shook his head, complaining of stomach pains and feeling sick and washed out.

"A couple of day's rest and I'll be good," he said walking into the lounge and flopping down on the sofa. I knew it was selfish, but I felt my stomach twist up. He would be hanging around here and I wouldn't be able to continue my mission in peace. I went to the kitchen and switched on the kettle, giving myself time to think and calm down.

"Aww thanks." Justin smiled taking the large cup of tea I had made him.

"No worries. How are you feeling?"

"Crappy, but nice to be home. It's been full on for weeks and I think I'm just burnt out." I nodded and told him about my visit to the doctor.

"I think that's a great idea. We could both do with spending more time together."

Again, my stomach dropped. It wasn't because I didn't want to...I loved him, but my sick leave wouldn't be used for the purpose I intended, and I felt irritated.

"Let's watch a movie," Justin suggested. I nodded, "Ok."

"I'll go shower first. You look at what to watch," he said getting up and heading upstairs. I wasn't interested, but I had no convincing excuse to refuse. After all, he was glad to have some time together and I couldn't complain at that. I heard the shower spring into life upstairs and I scrolled through the movie selection. Nothing grabbed my attention, and I looked half- heartedly. My phone buzzed beside me and the message wasn't from a number saved in my contacts. I unlocked the phone and stared in shock at the screen.

"*Stop looking.*

8

Justin lay on the sofa, yawning every few minutes in a dramatic way. He had been moaning about how tired he felt. It irritated me he was being blatantly fake. He wanted a lazy day, and to be honest it was fine with me. I could go and do what I wanted in peace.

"I'm going for a run," I called over my shoulder as I left the house. He mumbled something but didn't break his gaze from the TV. I ran towards town, passed the local secondary school before heading down the Billy line. My destination was Cavangh house. It had to be the link to all this. The muddy track seemed to go on for miles, trees hunched over like an arch in some places. A light drizzle of rain made my gym gear damp. A snap within the trees made me slow my pace. I scanned the area but there was nothing to see. It was silent again. I picked up my pace. After a few steps the noise replayed; a loud cracking sound that seemed to stay in time with my steps. I stopped and turn my head slowly. Sophia stared back at me from within the trees. Her finger pointed in the direction I was going and she slowly nodded her head. My legs powered forward until I reached the house. My heart was beating fast, but not with fear, but adrenaline.

The house creaked with every step, and dust filled the air causing my throat to dry up. I searched the house fully. It wasn't as terrifying in the daylight. I started upstairs. Four bedrooms, a large bathroom and a cupboard. There was nothing in the first two bedrooms but a couple old broken chairs and a grubby teddy bear. The bathroom was covered in mold, tiles missing from the walls and the toilet was brown. The smell was horrific. Old stale water from God knows when filled the bathtub. I couldn't stop the vomit from coming. The stench was so putrid, it burned my throat.

Something stuck out from the water. I bent down to inspect and stumbled backwards, screaming. I fell to the floor and continued to scream. A decomposed body floated in the bathtub. I crawled out of the room and sobbed. I hadn't looked enough to see any features, and I was scared to go back. Once outside, I retched again. The air wasn't enough to erase the smell. My hands shook as I dialed 999. I couldn't think about who that might be and blocked the thought that was clawing to get inside. Tears pricked at my eyes as I waited.

Several police officers approached, one knelt to my level. She had kind brown eyes and red hair pulled back into a bun. A few others entered the house, and I prepared for the impact of my discovery. After a few minutes had passed, suddenly, there was a rush of activity. They ushered me to a nearby police car. I watched in silence as more cars arrived and the police taped off the house. The kind police officer joined me in the back of the car and asked questions. Why was I in the house, was there anyone else with me? Did I touch anything?

"I used to mess about in that house as a kid. I was just intrigued to see it again. My friend has been missing for ten years, I just wanted to go back to somewhere that

I could remember her. I know that sounds weird."

I sounded unconvincing, crazy or both. Red bun nodded and wrote some notes. There was no expression on her face. She looked back at me and asked if I needed to call someone. I shook my head. I couldn't think straight let alone have a conversation.

"Sophia…" I whispered.

"Sorry, who?" The police officer asked putting down her notepad.

"Sophia is my missing friend. Is it her?"

"I don't know, but we will find out. I really think we should get someone to pick you up."

I handed her my phone, and she called Justin, I couldn't hold back the tears as my heart broke. I had found Sophia, I knew i

9

I didn't get out of bed for three days after they confirmed it was Sophia. I didn't eat, wash or speak. Ten years of not knowing, hoping, had now ended. Now, all I had was grief. I could finally let go, but I wouldn't, not yet. Sophia wasn't done, for those three days she'd sat in my room just staring. Nobody else could see her, but she never moved from the chair in the corner. Justin was growing more concerned as the days passed.

"Kim, you need to get up."

I didn't respond, just lay there like a mute. I felt nailed down, my brain was working but my body would not move. Is this what sheer grief feels like? I had always known she was dead; I couldn't understand the sense of loss. I had lost her ten years ago and I think it was finally hitting me. It shattered my mind into pieces. I wanted to die too. In that moment I could've happily faded away. It could be months before the investigation was completed and the murdering bastard was caught, if they ever were. The most upsetting thing for all of us who loved her was the fact it was proven Sophia had been pregnant when she was killed. Possibly three months...that was a key factor in the case. They needed to find out who the father was, but Sophia was seeing Lewis, so it was obvious. He had been in to give a DNA test the previous day.

It hurt that I knew nothing about such an important thing in her life. I almost felt betrayed that she hadn't trusted me enough. It was stupid to be angry with her, but I was, a little. I hadn't suspected a thing. She hadn't looked pregnant, but then again, she had been staying in more, and suddenly wearing jumpers a lot more than usual. I had just put it down to the winter.

"Kim, I need to go down to the station." Justin said breaking into my thoughts. I sat up, the first time in days.

"Why?" I asked, panic setting in.

"Don't worry, they want anyone who knew Sophia to give DNA samples. It is for the investigation. I won't be long."

It made sense to eliminate people from the investigation. Justin kissed my forehead and left the house. I heard the car pull out of the drive and fade into the distance. Sophia had gone, no longer in the room. It was almost unsettling...maybe that's why I felt so confused.

"Sophia?"' I called, but it was silent, her presence had gone. I forced myself out of bed and into the shower. I suddenly realized just how badly I needed on. No wonder my husband slept in the spare room the previous night. I felt dizzy at the lack of food and had to lie on the floor after leaving the shower. The hazy feeling passed after a few minutes, enough so I could get me dressed. A shower, clean hair and a bit of make-up can make a girl feel just a little better. I forced a slice of buttered toast down and a large cup of coffee. It helped, and then, I took a walk. The sun was bright that morning. A nice day also helped my mood.

I took a deep breath and let the fresh air fill my lungs. It was nice to be outside. I put in my earphones and turned the volume up to loud. The music helped me walk. Thirty minutes later, I approached the park in the centre of town. Families played in the kids' area. The screams of happy children echoed around me. A group of lads played football on the grass; their trousers all covered in grass stains. A normal sunny day with people smiling was almost enough to make me forget. I closed my eyes for a few seconds and listened to the sounds of the park. When I opened them again, I gasped and reeled back. I let out a scream as Sophia crawled along the ground. The rattle she made sounded like a snake, blood dripped from her fingers as they scraped along the floor. Her head turned to the side and a look of pure rage covered her face.

"My baby..." She hissed.

Her hand grabbed at my leg and I kicked out in panic. She looked so angry, I feared for my life. I couldn't help the hysterical screaming. A hand grabbed my arm and pulled me up from the dirt.

"Are you OK?" a father asked, he held his young son close to him. I took in my surroundings and it sunk in that only I had seen Sophia. The entire park had witnessed me having a complete meltdown over nothing. The feeling of humiliation overwhelmed me. I shrugged the kind man's hand off me and ran so fast out of the park. Onlookers watching me go with bewildered looks on their faces. I didn't stop until I was safely home. Only my day was about to get much worse, a car was parked in my drive and I knew who owed the silver BMW. The door opened and Lewis stepped out, he looked broken, his eyes were puffed from crying.

"Who's was it?" Lewis shouted as he stormed towards me. "You must know!"

I took a step back in fear. Lewis was positively raging. "I don't know what you're talking about."

He shook his head, taking another step towards me. He was shaking with anger. "How could she?"

I braved a step closer. "What's happened?"

"It wasn't my baby." Lewis sobbed.

"What?!"

"Don't pretend you didn't already know!" Lewis yelled, spittle dripped down his chin. "I have spent all this time mourning a girl who clearly didn't feel the same about me."

"I swear I don't know anything. I didn't know she was pregnant until now. I promise you Lewis, she told me nothing. I feel gutted she didn't trust me enough to tell me."

"You told each other everything." He said a calmer tone to his voice.

"Apparently not. I'm sorry. I...I don't know what to say." I held out my arms and he fell into them. I pulled him inside.

"Whiskey?" I offered. He nodded.

"I'll join you." I said and grabbed the bottle and glasses.

"I think we both need it."

We both sat in shocked silence as we processed the news. If Lewis wasn't the dad then who was?

"I feel so betrayed." Lewis was shocked to his core.

"She adored you," I tried to reassure him, but who could argue with the evidence.

"Really?!" He snapped, "She was a slag."

I couldn't stop myself from what I did next. I hit him so hard across the face I left a red mark.

"Don't you dare talk about her in that way. We have no idea what happened. She isn't here to defend herself." I was disgusted with him. I knew he was upset, I understood his anger, but until we knew exactly what had happened, turning on her was not acceptable.

"Whatever is the truth, she's still dead. Murdered, she didn't deserve that. Bad mouthing her isn't fair."

Lewis's face flushed red and he glared at me. "She was pregnant by someone else. She cheated on me and was having a baby. Forgive me for being a bit pissed off."

His head went down and he held it with both hands, "I'm sorry. I didn't mean it."

I knew it was the grief and shock talking. I hugged him so tight I thought my arms would break. My eyes lifted as I caught a movement and Sophia crouched before us.

"I'm sorry," she hissed before shrieking so loud a crack appeared in my TV, *"Tell him I am so sorry!"*

"What the hell?" Lewis said as he stared at the TV, the large crack visible.

"You need to listen to me," I said. "I, I...have been seeing Sophia."

Lewis stiffened beside me. "Are you fucking serious?"

I nodded.

"Why would you say such a thing?" His eyes narrowed and he frowned.

"Because it's true." I didn't like the way he looked at me. It was as if he didn't know me. "I don't understand it myself. She's always been trying to get through to me. I wasn't having breakdowns all these years...it was her." I waited for his response. He stood up and walked towards my door.

"Unbelievable," he scoffed, turning to face me. "Sophia is dead!" I watched Sophia behind him, a devastated look on her face; it twisted into despair and her body shook violently. She twisted and bent in ways no living person could have done.

"She's behind you. Stop you're upsetting her," I said.

"Kim, stop. I know you've not coped well, but that's going too far."

"She's sorry..."

"I can't listen to this any longer. I think the world of you Kim, but I can't deal with this right now. Get some help..." The door slammed as he left, and I was left staring at my front door hoping he'd come back. He didn't..

10

I knew I looked awful, the bags under my eyes were more like suitcases. I was exhausted after weeks of no sleep. Sophia was haunting me constantly, just watching me in silence. Sometimes her features were those I remember and other times it was darkness, anger and rage. Nobody listened to me, my own husband wouldn't discuss it anymore. He forced me back to the doctors, my sick note was extended for a further two weeks. I just wanted to see my mum, I missed my parents and I was heading to their house to surprise them. Usually I would plan it, but I decided it would be nice to see them without it being scheduled.

The radio blared and I tried to clear my mind, strangely Sophia hadn't appeared today. It was a huge relief and I looked forward to a cup of tea and an overdue chat with my mum. My parents still lived in Bedhampton in my childhood home. I passed The Golden Lion pub, and the small row of shops before arriving at their house. I smiled as I pulled into the drive.

Both cars were in the driveway. The cat, Pearl, a fluffy white Persian, sat inside perched on the windowsill keeping an eye on her domain. As I parked, she stood recognizing me. She was thirteen and had been a big part of all our lives. I realized I missed her. Knowing the front door would be locked, I headed for the back door. I slowly slid the patio door open, trying to sneak in without them noticing, only the shouting from upstairs made me freeze.

"How many times do we have to go over this?!" my dad's angry words filtered down the stairs.

"When you start telling me the truth," my mother's voice this time. She sounded off, her voice was full of hate, but there was something else. She sounded as if she was struggling to get her words out. I listened from where I stood in shock at the unfamiliar way my parents spoke to each other. It was so disconnected from what I knew. My mum began to scream obscenities at my dad, and it made my heart break. Pearl rubbed against my legs and meowed at me. I patted her head and watched her run out the patio doors.

"Don't touch me you fucking bastard! I wish I had never met you Dennis...Piss Off!"

"Christ woman, you need fucking help!"

The angry sound of my dad stomping angrily down the stairs got louder. I now stood in the living room completely still as he appeared through the door. He stopped, concern on his face. I wasn't supposed to hear any of that was what his expression told me.

"Kim, I didn't know you were coming today." He tried to sound relaxed, unphased by my arrival but he couldn't pull it off.

"I...I wanted to surprise you," I muttered.

"Lovely... Brew?" He offered heading for the kitchen. I nodded as I followed. There was a sound from upstairs and then light footsteps on the stairs. My mum joins us both and I was shocked to see how ill she looked. She'd lost weight, her hair was unkempt and she clearly hadn't been sleeping.

"What's wrong Mum?" I asked, she waved the comment away.

"I'm fine. I'm just getting over a cold. It really knocked me for six this one," she forced a smile. "I'm getting there so don't fuss."

It was all lies, and it stung a little that they were doing it to me. The kettle clicked as it came to the boil. My dad occupied the silence with the tea making, taking more time than was needed.

"How are things, darling?" Mum asked, taking my arm and leading me to the living room. There was an unsteadiness about her, and an odd smell. I couldn't put my finger on it in that moment. In fact, everything about my parents, even the house seemed off, out of kilter. The warm aura of the home I had grew up in wasn't detectable.

"What is going on?" I snapped, unable to stop the accusation. Mum tensed and avoided eye contact.

"I'm not well, I told you." There was irritation in her tone. I wasn't going to get a truthful answer I quickly realized. I excused myself, claiming I needed to pee. Once upstairs I took a proper look at the bedrooms. It was obvious they were not in the same room. All my dad's stuff was shoved in the spare room with a single bed, it was unmade. I felt like a child, the heart break crashed over me like an angry ocean. They were in trouble and I knew it. I turned back and stomped back down to the kitchen.

"Don't lie to me. What is going on with you and Mum?" My dad stopped stirring the tea, but didn't look at me.

"Your mum isn't doing so well. I'm sorting it, it's going to be fine. I promise."

What did he mean by that? Thoughts raced around my mind. All kinds of scary illnesses sprung to mind. I began to panic until my mum appeared, staggering towards me and it all fell into place. Clutching a vodka bottle she stumbled into the wall. "The only...problem... is this piece of shit." Her words were slurred, drawn out and full of venom as she jabbed a finger in my Dad's direction.

"Mum!" Fury rose in me. How could she speak to him like that, "What is wrong with you?"

"Him," she snarled. "It's all his fault!"

"Dad?" He looked at me finally with emptiness in his eyes. The strong man I always ran to when I needed help wasn't what I saw. His usual strong presence had been sucked away.

"She doesn't mean it. It's the drink."

My mother was an alcoholic, and it would appear my Dad had been dealing with it in secret.

"Why didn't you tell me?"

He took in a deep breath and pulled me to him, hugging me so tight it almost felt safe. I wasn't safe, none of us were. My parents were falling apart.

"Don't touch her!" My mum screamed, pulling at my arm to separate us. "Get off my baby!" Her cries were desperate, bordering on hysterical. "Give her to me, stay away. You won't take her from me."

I tried to calm her, reassure her that wasn't what was happening, but I wasn't dealing with the loving women I knew as my mum. This was someone else, a confused and very sick version of her.

"He isn't taking me away, you need to calm down. Please, you need help."

"I don't need help. I need him to fuck off. I can't do this anymore!"

I look at my dad and he shrugs.

"I don't know what I have done wrong, this has been going on for years."

My mum finished the bottle before slumping to the floor, my dad caught her before she hit her head. I watched in a daze as he carried her lovingly up the stairs, tucking her safely into bed.

"She'll be out for the count for a few hours," he said afterwards. He stood looking at me as he tried to find the words to say next. There were no words but a river of tears as he finally let it all out. It was my turn to take care of him. I held him as he confessed the extent of her problem. It started years ago, slowly at first, he just thought it was stress from her job back then.

"She hated that place, dealing with so much shit from the public. Customer service can be brutal. Then when Sophia went missing, she was so worried about you, it impacted."

It had been over ten years, gradually getting out of control. "She went through stages of being OK, but lately it is so much worse. I don't know why she hates me so much. I haven't done anything."

He had tried to get her help, but she refused to accept any. She claims she doesn't have a problem with drinking.

"Until she admits it, I can't help her. She'll wake up and won't remember a thing about what just happened. It'll be the old Kathy, and I can't bring myself to tell her otherwise."

"Oh Dad, I'm so sorry." I held him while he cried on my shoulder. "I'm here now. You are not alone."

"I didn't want you to see her like this. I wanted to protect you, and her."

It didn't stop the feeling of guilt knowing he had been dealing with this alone.

11

I looked at the messages in the group chat, taking my time to respond. Apps had become the way we communicated these days. Private chats seemed uncommon. Constant notifications distracting you from doing anything important. I hated it all, but was still as guilty as the rest of the world for needing a phone in my hand every five seconds. Chloe was arranging a catch up before everyone headed back to their normal lives. The mourning period for Sophia was coming to an end for most of us. They needed to get back to work. Adam responded next.

"Sorry guys, I've got to get back to Japan. Flight is later this afternoon. Next time, I promise. Take care of yourselves."

I should go. These were my oldest friends, but I wasn't in a sociable mood. I knew I had to, reluctantly I replied saying we would see them tomorrow. Justin was excited and I couldn't spoil it for him.

"It'll be good for us all." Justin tried to

make it sound like a good night out, but Sophia's memory would still be hanging over us. I forced a smiled and focused on getting dinner ready. Justin planted a kiss on my cheek as he passed me, happy that I had agreed. He pulled a bottle of Prosecco from the fridge and waved it at me.

"Yeah, go on," I replied. He set the table and poured the wine. It had been weeks since we had sat down together for dinner, and I realized I had pushed Justin away. I needed to focus on us for a night...I owed him that.

"Smells great," Justin smiled, taking a sip of wine. I suddenly noticed him, the handsome man I married. I realized I missed him and the closeness we once had. I gave him a genuine smile as I stirred the chicken risotto. I took out two plates and piled Justin's plate high adding some homemade bread to the side. I wasn't as hungry, so mine looked like a child's portion compared to his. I blanked out Sophia, it was our time now. We chatted and I discussed my worries about mum.

"I had no idea. That must have been hard to witness. It explains how odd they've been." Justin held my hand tightly.

"She'll be OK," he whispered, kissing my forehead. "You know now, we can support them both. We will get her the help she needs."

That was why I loved him, always doing everything to make things better. I was hit with guilt at my lack of appreciation for him. "I'm sorry I have been such a wreck."

There were tears in his eyes, "You lost your best friend; we lost a friend. You two were more like sisters and I don't blame you for grieving. I just worry that you aren't coping." He was referring to my visions of Sophia as he called them. I let it go to avoid another fall out.

"It hasn't been the best these past few weeks," I agreed. Once we had finished dinner, Justin cleaned up while I settled on the sofa. Friday nights were not the same as when we were younger. It was all about clubbing and getting smashed. Now, unless we had a specific place to be, a bottle of wine and a good movie was heaven. I perused the movie selections while the clinking of dishes from the kitchen echoed through the walls. Justin whistled loudly sounding the most relaxed he had been in weeks.

"Do we have any chocolate?" I yelled, the need for something sweet with my wine had taken over. A short silence met my question before he appeared with a packet of Chocolate digestive biscuits in his hand.

"Yes," I cheered.

"It's all we have, but it will do." Justin handed me the packet, kissing my lips as he did so.

"I love you, you know that, right?" I nodded, I did. Suddenly I felt so lonely. His kiss had stirred something, and I grabbed him. Our lips locking desperately, the movie abandoned.

Later after session three, a record only beaten by our wedding night, I rested my head on Justin's chest. The beating of his heart was almost hypnotic. He kissed my head repeatedly in gratitude for fulfilling his male need. Something I had deprived him of for several months. He never complained, but the puppy dog eyes when I refused repeatedly was enough to know. Sleep was taking hold, my eyes were closing and that feeling of being safe wrapped in my husband's arms, was making me more relaxed when the noise broke my safe place.

Crash, Crash...

"What the fuck?" Justin jumped up, telling me to stay in bedroom. I watched him leave, crouched over walking as silently as possible. It sounded like it was in the kitchen. Metal was banging and the clatter of cutlery hitting a hard surface like a cascade of breaking ice. It was so loud and piercing in the darkness.

"Who the fuck is in our house?! Piece of shit come and show yourself," I heard Justin's angry, but tense voice. I feared he might be attacked and went to find him. He stood in the kitchen, shaking his head as he called 999. Our kitchen looked ransacked. Saucepans, cutlery, plates and food scattered all over the floor. A bottle of tomato ketchup had been smashed and along the wall were the words: "Please, Listen. Nobody ever listens."

Justin turns as a cracking sound from behind us fills the room. His eyes widen and his skin goes pale.

" Sophia?" He gasps. "No..." He looks at me, terror and confusion in his expression, "My God, you were telling the truth!"

Finally, he believed me! He knew I wasn't going insane. He scrambled backwards, a rolling pin causing him to lose his balance. I watched as his head smashed against the counter and the crack from his skull made my stomach clench, it was sickening. He hit the floor, a crumpled heap. There was no movement or sound and blood oozed from the back of his head.

"No!" I screamed, "No!

12

This must be a dream...it can't be real. The seats were all taken, and a hushed mutter of voices surrounded me. Dad held my hand tightly. No, it's not happening, but the vicar began to speak. He talked about Justin and how he will be missed. I still don't believe any of it. I'll wake up soon from this nightmare. I need to wake up, but I don't. The casket before me couldn't contain my soul mate because I needed him. He promised me so much! He promised we would grow old together, have children, and they would have kids of their own.

Sophia hunched over him, her hand on the casket. I could hear her sobs.

"I didn't mean it. I just wanted him to see," she whispered, a low sound that seemed to filter only to my ears. *"But I needed you to hear me."*

In my grief, my loyalty to her began to fade. "Why?" I screamed. "Why take him, he didn't do anything wrong!"

I was screaming now and completely lost my composure. My dad wrestled with me as I continued my breakdown. It was only after I insulted anyone in my eyeline, mainly the poor vicar did I realize what I had done. I wasn't screaming at Sophia anymore. She'd gone, again. I hated the pitying looks from the near hundred people in attendance. It was all too much to cope with, but I had to get through the service for Justin's sake. I was angry with the world and everyone in it. My mother especially, too drunk to attend. My dad gave excuses for her but we both knew instead of supporting me, she'd hit the bottle instead. Selfish cow.

All I wanted to know was who had killed Sophia, now more than ever. Her presence was increasing, and I had lost my husband because of it. It was all I could think of now. Justin would still be here. He wouldn't be dead if Sophia were alive. Whoever this person was had caused his death and my pain was morphing into pure rage. Walking past his casket was the hardest part, leaving him behind, alone. Christmas was approaching and it held no meaning for me anymore.

The day passed in a blur...I nodded in the right places or at least that's what I hoped I was doing. I hadn't noticed Yvonne at the service, but she was approaching me now. The look of pity, and of knowing my pain.

"Kim, I am so sorry."

I let her embrace me, but I said nothing. Her daughter had done this, her dead daughter. I held my tongue because it wasn't her fault. We took a seat and she handed me a glass of vodka and lemonade.

"I'm here if you need anything." Yvonne said. My barrier came down a little; being angry is exhausting. "Thanks."

We chatted, more small talk if I'm honest but then she mentioned the photos. "You did get them I assume?"

It had completely slipped my mind. I never went back to pick up the pictures from the memory box. I can't believe I forgot. That would be a job for tomorrow.

The drinks continued to flow and hushed voices grew louder as people began to exchange stories of Justin. Laughter at times, it made me smile briefly until the pain tore at what remained of my heart. Yvonne eventually left and Chloe replaced her.

"I can't believe this is happening, babe. Do you need anything?"

She had been the only person from our group to attend. Adam couldn't get back in time, Matt had come down with a horrible sickness bug and couldn't leave the bathroom, apparently. Lewis hadn't returned any of my calls. It hurt so much that he hadn't been in contact, just showed me he didn't care anymore. I was still accused of something I hadn't done. Lewis can go fuck himself as far as I was concerned. Justin had been his friend, and I thought Lewis would be a better person and put that to one side for the sake of a friend. I was clearly so very wrong.

"Can you bring him back?" I snapped

and instantly regretted it. "Sorry, ignore that."

"I wish I could, he was one of the good guys." She'd been crying, her make-up was smudged.

It was true, he was.

"I miss him so much," I broke into sobs... Chloe caught me before I fell from the chair.

"I know. I've got you sweetheart. I'm going to stay for a while." Her flight back to LA was due that evening but she decided not to go back to Chris.

"You don't have to; you have your own life to live," I mumbled. Her expression showed defiance.

"Chris can wait. He's stuck in studios lately anyway." I noticed the tone of her voice, not normal for her. She sounded irritated when saying his name. I had more important things to worry about, so I didn't question it. Chloe stayed by my side the entire day, showing she was the friend she claimed to be. I was glad to be home later that night. Although the house didn't feel the same, it felt empty and cold. Justin's jacket hung at the bottom of the stairs. I couldn't move it, not yet. Chloe had left to check into a hotel, I should offer my spare room, but I needed some space, to cry without an audience. Maybe, tomorrow I will want the company.

I walked around the house, like a lost child. Nothing felt comforting. It was alien to me, and I no longer wanted to be there. I sat in the chair, looking out of my lounge window and watched the world carry on as if nothing had changed. It hadn't for them, but for me - life had stopped. My best friend and husband were dead, and my mother had a drinking problem. This was causing my parents to fall apart. In short, my life was shit. I couldn't take the pain any longer, I wanted to forget it all.

Several bottles of Vodka sat in the kitchen, and I made my way there. I don't remember much after that.

I woke the next day on my kitchen floor, cold and covered in my own vomit. The headache hit me full on, forcing me back into the fetal position. I wasn't getting up anytime soon. My eyesight was blurred, but the dragging sound was loud and clear.

Scratching was next and getting closer and then a movement to my right. A hand reached through the kitchen door. It was black and blue, rotting and the smell made me vomit over myself again. The rattlesnake sound made me freeze in fear. I hated it when she made that noise.

"Sophia, just stop." I begged.

"No..." I felt the cold grip on my arm, I was flipped upwards and thrown across the kitchen.

Sophia held her rotting hand against my forehead forcing my head back against the wall. I couldn't move and my surroundings blurred and melted away.

13

I was standing in Sophia's bedroom. She was crying as she frantically typed something on her phone. After a few exchanges she grabbed her coat and left the house. A quick look behind her and she charged through the door like there was a fire...panic in her eyes. I followed with anticipation as to what information I could get from this. I followed her from Bedhampton down to the train station, crossed over the bridge and headed towards the industrial estate. She seemed to fade a little as she got further away. She turned into a carpark surrounded by various units. It must have been a weekend as it was deserted. I scanned the area and saw the back of Sophia's head. She stood talking to someone. The darkness shaded who it was, but her body language was one of stress or anger maybe both. A few steps took me closer, and I could pick up a few words.

"I'm sorry, I needed you!"

"We have discussed what you need to do, Sophia. We need to get this sorted. I can't keep doing this. I can't bare the lies anymore."

I felt sick. I knew that voice. It couldn't be, I had to be mistaken. I wanted to run away, but my feet took over and I was walking forward. His face came into view and my stomach twisted, it felt like the bottom had just fallen from my entire world.

My dad had his hand on her arm, his face close to hers.

"Seriously, this needs to be between us. Nobody else," Sophia made him promise. "Nobody can ever know."

I screamed and I was catapulted backwards, and I woke up on my kitchen floor. I was back to reality but feeling even more devastated.

What was that? I ran to the toilet and threw-up several times. The thoughts flew around my mind, trying to find a logical, innocent reason for what I had seen. My gut feeling was it wasn't a simple explanation. My dad had looked so intense...so frightened. No, he wouldn't do that, he wouldn't! He loved my mother, he wouldn't cheat on her, not with anyone and certainly not with my best friend.

"Sophia, please tell me it isn't what I think!" I screamed, causing more vomiting.

My mothers' drunken rantings suddenly made sense. Then the hammer blow of realization. If Lewis wasn't the baby's father, was it my dad?

I needed to find out but if it was what I feared, I wasn't sure I could handle it. It was all just too much, and my depression was circling me like a vulture. I couldn't allow it to take hold of me. I counted to ten and buried it deep down and crawled into bed. The exhaustion finally took over and sleep came easy. Sleeping meant I couldn't feel the pain and my heart breaking into a thousand pieces.

I woke later than usual the next morning; it was gone eleven. I didn't allow my mind to think of anything other than getting out and picking up the mystery photos. I hoped it would show something else, or someone else to investigate. I needed to erase any doubt I had about my dad. I knew ignoring it wasn't going to change what I had seen, but it helps even if it was temporary. Anything to push my grief as far down as possible and block any thought of Justin.

The traffic was chaos. Eventually I parked and headed towards Boots only stopping at Costa to grab a hot chocolate. I cursed myself at not thinking about the shoppers, I hadn't even thought about the fact it was two days before Christmas. Getting anything quickly wasn't possible. I clutched my hot drink with gloved hands and waited in line for the photos. A ranting customer wanting the pictures from his daughter's wedding was causing a delay. A manager was called and finally after a heated argument, the missing order was found making the wait speed up.

I handed over my receipt and began to feel a little nervous as the pictures were handed to me. Once back in my car, I slowly drank my hot chocolate putting off the task at hand. I didn't know why I was so terrified. The unknown had a knack at picking at anxiety. My hands shook as I opened the envelope. The pile of photos was heavy in my hand. I looked at the first one and it made me smile for second, and then I cried.

The faces of my friends all huddled together... me in the middle. Taken earlier in the evening, we were happy. The next was Sophia and me in a hug on the dancefloor. I got lost in the memories. All these pictures were wonderful moments before she vanished. Maybe, there wasn't anything sinister about the camera. I could have forgotten I had put it in the box, and that made me feel a bit relieved. Some nice thoughts were needed.

I headed home and the thoughts about my dad pushed their way into my mind. It needed discussing sooner rather than later. I'd spend the remainder of the day resting, allow myself to cry for my husband. He deserved that.

I turned up the heat in my cold house and wrapped myself in a blanket. A bottle of white wine and a cheese sandwich was all I needed. Sipping slowly from my glass, I flicked through the pictures again. My heart bursting with love for my friends and breaking for the loss of two. After a long and ugly cry, I felt myself relax. It was a release of pressure; one I so badly needed. I was drifting off when I felt a whip of air. My hair flared out and the pictures floated from my hands. Most landed face down, but two were face up. I didn't have to look up, I knew Sophia was in the room.

"I can't take anymore." I sighed. "No more."

"Look!"

Slowly I reached for the two photos. At first, I didn't see anything other than party memories. The first was me and Justin, arms around each other with smiles, the other was the same picture with an added face. Chloe was part of our huddle.

"I don't understand..."

Sophia was barely visible, more like a mist. She seemed weak, *"Keep looking."*

I did, over and over to the point my eyes hurt. Sophia's presence was less intense, but I knew she was watching me. "I'm being forgotten," her voice was full of despair. "You must help me! I just want to rest. I want to stop feeling this pain, anger and betrayal."

"Just tell me."

"I can't, I just can't."

My eyes noticed something. It hadn't been obvious, but in the background of each photo was something odd. Adam and Sophia. His expression was angry as he looked at her. His hand gripped hers. They were in a heated debate about something.

"Adam?"

What possible reason would her shy, kind friend have to be angry with Sophia. I had more questions now, and no answers and I had been left alone to ponder on them. I was used to having my dead friend appear now and I no longer feared it; it wasn't normal. Maybe I wasn't normal, sometimes I did consider all this was in my head. I had to talk to Adam, without thinking I was calling his number. The dead dial tone threw me, I must have misdialled. Several attempts gave the same outcome. I went to WhatsApp and opened the group chat.

Adam has left the chat. What was going on, I sent a message.

"Why has Adam left the group?" A few seconds passed and Matt replied. "That's odd, I've no idea."

Everyone was confused. "Is he OK?" Chloe asked.

I didn't mention the pictures. I couldn't bring that up, not yet. Maybe his phone was broken...or lost. A perfectly simple explanation. I hoped it was that. He could not be part of this. My gut feeling was telling me different, but I tried to ignore it. I was blocking a lot from my mind. I should be grieving for Justin, but I felt numb. No emotion...just empty. I couldn't cry or even think about him. I searched for Adam on Facebook; he was still there on my friend list. I sent a friendly message asking how he was. He didn't reply straight away, but when he did, he confirmed he was fine, and leaving the group chat hadn't been deliberate.

That was a relief, for a second. I thought I had lost another friend. Shortly after I re-added him. He sent a funny message and we moved on. But he was not his usual chatty self. Longer delays in his replies and shorter responses made me feel like the bond we all used to have was slowly fading away.

14

I couldn't breathe...hands gripped my neck.

I felt the nails digging into my skin.

Opening my eyes, trying to see who was attacking me was more terrifying than the attack itself. There was no face, just an empty black void. I tried to fight back but I was overpowered. A sense of rage wrapped around me; the attack became frenzied, manic even. The pain as my head hit something hard vibrated my whole body. My vison became blurred and tears stung my eyes as my skull felt shattered into pieces.

"Stop, please," I begged.

I kicked out and the weight of my attacker disappeared. I rolled over and fell to the floor. I jolted awake, sweat poured from me. Another nightmare, it was the same one as the previous three nights. My phone was ringing on the bedside table.

"Merry Christmas!" my mother sang. Her voice was joyful and slurry. I checked the time and it was only ten in the morning. Saying anything would only start an argument and it was Christmas day, I didn't want that. '

"Merry Christmas to you to Mum."

I could hear liquid pouring as she topped the glass up.

"What time are you getting here?" My mother asked. I wanted to say I wasn't. As far as I was concerned, Christmas was cancelled this year. I hadn't prepared at all. Nobody would be receiving presents or cards. I would have dinner with my parents and head home. Sitting in the same room as my Dad was going to be hard after my vision the other night. The messages ping through on my phone with cheery festive spirit. I had none, so I didn't reply.

A few hours later, I was sitting in the kitchen of my childhood home watching my mum pretend to be sober and painfully try to cook the best Christmas dinner anyone would have in this country. So she claimed. Yeah, she was drunk. My dad fussed around me ensuring I had a drink or a snack while I waited. The feeling of disgust was rising and getting harder to hold back.

"You look very pale," Dad commented, concern in his eyes.

"My best friend and Husband are both dead. I'm hardly having the best time," I snapped. He looked hurt but didn't respond. A pang of guilt hit me and I saw the stress in my dad's eyes.

"I know, we miss him too." He held my hand and I knew he saw Justin as a son. He was devastated over his death. The daughter in me needed her Dad. He had always been my rock, my hero. He couldn't have done anything bad. No, he wouldn't.

"Have you heard anymore from Lewis?" My mother suddenly asked. I shook my head.

"Nope."

I was still pissed off he didn't attend Justin's funeral. Heartbroken was more the feeling. "He didn't bother to show up for Justin's funeral, so he's shown me exactly how he feels." The bitterness tainted each of my words.

"Can you blame him after what she did? And...," my mum said sharply, slamming a pan down on the side.

"What?!" I rose from my seat.

"Nothing."

"It was something. Come on, don't hold back Mum."

Another sip of her wine before she turned to look at me. "I simply meant Lewis has every right to be angry." I didn't miss the glare she pointed towards my dad. "He has grieved for her and he finds out she was pregnant with someone else's baby. Maybe she wasn't the girl we all thought she was."

The tone in her voice didn't hide her disgust. "I think it's time we all moved on." I slammed my hand down on the table, sending my glass flying off the side. "She was my best friend, who was murdered. How can you be so fucking cold?"

I wanted to push the issue. Did my mum know something? It hit me! Looking back over the years, mum had never really been too involved. She helped in the first week to look for her and comforted me, but it eased off quicker than it did for most people. I had put it down to her concentrating on me, but I now began to question it. Did she know or suspect something back then and her disappearance was convenient for her? My dad had said nothing during this exchange, only watching with sadness at our tension.

"It's Christmas. Let's not fall out over it," he finally said, standing up and walking towards my mum. "Your mother is right. It's time you moved forward." His hand held his wife's and she relaxed. She even managed to smile at him. There was an odd feel in the air, my parents were not themselves. I could see it clearly now. They hadn't been right for a long time.

The day dragged on and we pretended to have a loving family Christmas, but I couldn't wait to get out of there. As it turned to evening, I called a taxi.

"It's been lovely, so nice to be together," my mother slurred as she leant against the wall. Not once had she asked about Justin or mentioned him. I was almost convinced he never existed. All she cared about was putting on a show while grasping at the last shred of a family we had left.

"Justin wasn't here, so it wasn't all that great," I couldn't help myself from saying it. The hurt on her face didn't phase me.

"Oh darling, we miss him to."

"Really?" I said sarcastically. "It seems like you've forgotten him." Her eyes widen in horror.   "Of course not. I didn't want to upset you."

I laughed out loud at the audacity. "But slagging my dead best friend off is OK? Go have another fucking drink. Here is something you should hear; you need to get some help."

My dad came striding down the hall. "Don't speak to your mother like that. She was only speaking the truth." I took a step back; he had changed his attitude very quickly.

"'Wow, I see. I am speaking the truth too. She's an alcoholic and needs professional help. Stop burying your head in the sand Dad. You know, these past few years have been crap, and she hasn't really helped me. Now, my husband is dead, and she thinks pretending he never existed won't upset me. It does, I'm a mess. But just go and fucking drink and pretend everything is fine. Our family is broken, and nothing will be changed until we face that fact."

I turned on my heels and opened the front door, the taxi sat waiting. "One other thing, I'm getting close to the truth about Sophia. I won't stop until I do. When I find those responsible, they will be brought to justice. Sophia didn't deserve this and neither did Justin."

Both faces of my parents were pale with hurt, guilt or both I wasn't sure. They stood like statues as I stomped to the waiting car. As I shut my front door behind me, I collapsed to the floor a broken woman with nothing else to give but cry myself to sleep. It was several days before I emerged from my bed properly.

15

Chloe pushed her way inside despite my protests. She wasn't happy after cancelling her flight back to LA and then I avoided her.

"I'm not going away, so stop being such an ignorant cow," she scolded, shrugging her coat off. "I know you're grieving and shit but hiding away isn't helping you. I'm here and you will bloody well talk to me."

I stood awkwardly in the leggings and t-shirt I had been wearing for days.

"You look like shit," Chloe commented. "No offense." I didn't take any.

"I feel like shit."

She held her arms out to me and I went in for the hug.

"When was the last time you ate? Or showered?" I shrugged. Chloe went into mother mode. I was showered, dressed, and hair done a few hours later.

"It doesn't change anything I know, but at least you look better," Chloe smiled warmly. She made us pasta and strong

107

coffee. I was happy she had barged her way in, I needed the company of somebody I trusted. Sophia's absence made me consider the reality of it. Did it really happen, had I imagined it all? I needed to get it out, talk to someone.

"I need to talk to you. Things are crazy and I need your opinion."

This had peaked her attention, taking a sip of her coffee she gestured for me to talk. I started off nervous, tripping over my words. As I spoke about seeing Sophia; I waited for the pity look, sympathy for crazy Kim. Instead the colour drained from her face. Her coffee mug slowly returned to the table.

"You think I've lost my mind, don't you? No worries, I'm used to that."

Chloe frantically shook her head. "No, I thought I was," she grabbed for my hand, her grip like a vice. "This past week...that is all I have seen. Sophia, in the mirror, at a distance when I'm walking down the street. Last night I woke to her staring at me, sitting in the chair of my hotel room."

The relief poured from me, and everything came out. I couldn't stop once I began. For the first time, somebody listened intently with no concern or scramble for my therapist's number.

"Justin died because he saw her. He slipped in shock?" Chloe asked.

I nodded and burst into tears, the memory flooded my mind. "For a split second he finally believed me. Then he was gone."

"My God, I'm so sorry. And you couldn't exactly tell people he'd died after seeing your dead friend. No wonder you've been a mess."

I had held back one part of my story, my suspicion about my dad. I felt ashamed at the thought and was scared to hear Chloe's thoughts on it. She eyed me, a knowing look on her face.

"There is something else, isn't there?" My eyes widened with shock. "Come on, how long have we known each other. I know when you're holding back." She finished her coffee and pushed the mug away, folding her hands in front of her. "I see Sophia too, so what can be worse than that?"

I sighed and put my head on the

table, "I'm so exhausted by all this. I feel my heart breaking over and over. I can't deal with this too."

"Deal with what?"

I sit up and look her in the eyes. "I think my dad is involved somehow." There I had said it, those words out loud. Chloe let out a gasp.

"What?!" Her eyes widened. "No way!"

"Unfortunately, I think he is." I explain about the vision, and how odd my parents were acting.

"Shit...maybe it was just a nightmare," Chloe suggested. "Stress can do that."

"No, it wasn't. There something going on between my parents. My Mum is ... is..." Chloe's eyes narrowed, "Is your Mum OK?" The concern in her voice was genuine.

"Yes and no. She's an alcoholic."

"Shut the fuck up! Your Mum?" I nodded and told her all about my recent experience of seeing my mum so drunk it was devastating. "She didn't come to Justin's funeral because she preferred to get shitfaced instead." The bitterness was to raw hide. "Maybe her problem is because of my dad."

The smash was so loud it made my eardrums vibrate. Chloe screamed like a four-year-old and nearly fell from her chair.

"I think I have just had a bloody heart attack," Chloe held her hand to her chest. "What was that?"

We ran towards the sound, my living room. The sofa had been overturned and the TV was in the middle of the room, smashed to pieces. The rattle from the corner vibrated, turning to a rumbling sound. My eyes fell on the hunched over shape, hair over the face. Skin so stretched and rotting the smell reached me from across the room. Chloe screamed. Sophia's head lifted sharply, one blood red eye peaked through the ratty hair.

"You need to hear the truth?" Her hand reached out to me. *"I need to be heard."*

She crawled slowly across the floor, on all fours. Like a predator stalking their pray. Her focus on me. *"I'm so sorry, tell him I'm sorry."*

I tried to back away, but her movement quickened, and she grabbed my ankle. I fell to the floor and she crawled upwards towards my face. Once our faces stared at each other Sophia opened her mouth. Blood dripped out covering my face.

"I can't rest …"

I looked to Chloe for help, but the fear had frozen her to the spot. Typical, she'd always been useless in a crisis.

Sophia flipped upwards and she hung from the ceiling on all fours, her head twisting round to glare at me. The cracking of her neck was loud, making me cringe.

"Please Soph! I can't take anymore. Stop!"

The rage erupted from my best friend like a volcano. The blood curdling cry vibrated around the house. The house began to shake and I thought it would crumble around us. Chloe grabbed my arm and pulled me to my feet. We ran through the patio doors into the garden. We were not safe, she followed like a Lioness tracking her pray, circling with prowess.

"He needs to know the truth," she hissed. *"I'm sick of being ignored, judged or worst of all...forgotten."*

She vanished and the atmosphere returned to normal. The cold December air freezing my skin. We went back inside the house and I threw on a baggy jumper to warm up.

"What do we do?" Chloe whispered. Shaken to her core, she struggled to catch her breath. I knew what we needed to do. There were, in fact, several things that needed to be done.

16

I didn't knock when I arrived at my
parents. I didn't want to give them time to
cover anything. My mother was sitting in
the kitchen, bottle of Vodka in her hand
and a cigarette. Oh, she'd started that
again, just brilliant. I assumed my dad was
upstairs. I grabbed the bottle from her
hand and threw it across the room. Her
reflex wasn't quick enough.

"What the hell are you doing?!" She
yelled, shock and anger on her face. Her
hand stretched out as if to save her drink.

"Start talking Mum," I could feel
myself getting hot as the adrenaline raced
through me. "Come on, why the
drinking?"

Her back turned to me and she
staggered towards the kitchen door, "I
don't have to explain myself to you. I like a
drink! You and him," her finger jabbed
towards the stairs "can just deal with it."

"What happened? You used to be so
happy." Her reaction was nothing short of
disgust.

"Yeah, well, things change." I didn't

114

like her nasty tone. I realized she'd been slowly getting worse. I'd not had the same relationship with her for a very long time. In her eyes, I saw pain and the unhappiness was so clear now.

"What did Dad do that was so bad...that you hate him so much?" Tears escaped her eyes and she dabbed them with her hands. "Things just break sometimes. Life kicks you in the teeth and sometimes it can't be fixed."

It wasn't an answer, but her tone had softened. "I'm so sorry Kim, for not being the mother you needed. I'm so sorry for the mess I have become." The anger drained from me as I watched her crumble like a child in front of me. I wrapped my arms around her. "Talk to me."

"What's going on?" My dad had heard the commotion from upstairs. "Everything OK?"

I shook my head. "I think it's time you both started being honest with me."

He sighed heavily, "I have tried to help her. I don't know why she hates me so much. I think the drinking is just destroying her."

It was like getting blood from a stone with these two. I started to question if they even knew what the problem between them was. I was about to interrogate my Dad about Sophia when the doorbell went. My mother muttered under her breath as she made her way to answer it. I stood looking at my Dad, we both looked defeated.

"She needs help. I've tried to keep this hidden for her sake. I can't anymore..."

We heard voices and then footsteps approaching. A radio sounded and two police officers entered the kitchen.

"Mr. Jennings, We need you to answer a few questions regarding Sophia's death."

My heart hammered in my chest.

"Me? Why?"

"It might be better if you accompanied us to the station," the male police officer politely suggested.

"I don't understand," my dad had no colour left to his skin. The confusion was evident. "What could I possibly tell you that you don't already know? I gave all the information I had back when she went missing ten years ago."

My mother snorted, a smug glare on her face.

"Please, Mr. Jennings. It would be better for you if you do." I patted his arm, "Dad, go…Just tell them again." He caught my eye and looked utterly petrified, "I don't know anything."

I watched him leave and get into the back of the police car. He hadn't been arrested but just helping with police inquiries, but I knew something bad was happening and I felt sick. As the car pulled out of the drive, I saw her standing under the tree opposite the house. She followed the car with her eyes with sadness. She whipped her head back to look at me, her face twisting into pure fury.

"No…," my mother gasped behind me. "Go away, leave us alone. Stay away." She was hysterical and when I studied her, I realized she could see Sophia and that was who she was screaming at. I was yanked back into the house, and she frantically locked the door as if that could stop her.

"Kim, did you see her?"

"Yes, I see her all the time." This shocked her which muted her for a second, her bottom lip quivered. "What?"

I pointed to the door, "That's not going to stop her."

My mother was shaking violently, her hands covering her chest. "What does she want?"

"The truth to come out. She may have died but she hasn't left. She is the reason Justin is dead." Our eyes locked and my mother broke down, this was the first time she had shown that kind of emotion over Justin. "I don't understand."

I explained what really happened that day, and what lead up to it. "Oh darling, I'm so sorry," her hand reached out to hold my hand, but I pulled away.

"What has Dad done?"

Her face became stone, no response. She had shut down, again. Like a sulky teenager she stomped upstairs, I followed her with fury boiling up inside.

"What are you hiding?"

"Leave it alone Kim, I can't do this right now."

She wouldn't look at me; her back stayed turned to me as we entered her bedroom.

"I think the time for avoiding this has passed. Dad has been sleeping in the spare room and no happily married couple sleeps separately."

Her head whipped back, her laugh was bitter and cold. "Happy...that was a long time ago." I ignored that comment.

"Sophia is here for a reason."

"Don't speak her name. I'm sick of hearing it." The venom in her voice shocked me. It was seconds later that the crashing sound interrupted her rant. It sounded like a bull crashing around. We ran from the room and back down the stairs, the sound continued until my Mum flew through the door. I was seconds behind her but her sudden stop sent me crashing into her.

"Ouch," I cried as my forehead collided with the back of her head. She didn't flinch, her body was rigid. "Mum," I tapped her shoulder, but she didn't respond. I moved looking into the room. I gasped at the sight. It had been destroyed.

Sofa's upturned and pictures smashed on the floor. The words written on the wall in what looked like blood, sent shivers down my spine.

I won't rest or forget.

I didn't deserve this.

I watched the slick red substance drip down the wall. The rattle came from behind us, turning I was face to face with Sophia. The cold whipped my black curls around my face; a breeze that wasn't possible.

"They'll tell lies." Her glare tore through my soul so full of pain, despair, sadness and rage.

"Run," my mother cried heading to the door. Sophia threw out her hand, her arm outstretched, and the door shut violently.

"Nobody leaves. They have to pay," Sophia hissed, her voice dry and cracked with each word. Water dripped from her dress, her party dress. *"Can't breathe,"* she sputtered, her hands around her throat. Water spilled from her mouth before she vanished before our eyes.

"No, it can't be," Mother sobbed as

she collapsed to her knees.

I was shaking so much I couldn't move, this time Sophia had been more menacing. There was nothing in her eyes, empty voids and I feared any part of her kind soul had gone. My best friend had suffered something terrible and she was angry, lost and stuck. You couldn't blame her. As a kid you would hear ghost stories, but you never really thought they existed, or at least hoped they didn't. I knew better. The worst ghost was my best friend. Her life cut short, never growing up and fulfilling all her hopes and dreams. Her unborn child had also died with her, another reason for her rage. My parents were involved somehow, and it made me sick. She deserved justice and her right to rest in peace. I had to face it. My dad had killed her because he'd gotten her pregnant. It was obvious, and Sophia wanted me to know, but I had to work it out for myself.

"Come on," I said, as I stood holding my hand out to my Mum. I felt guilty for allowing her to suffer alone. I embraced her and she sobbed into my chest. "It was

Dad, wasn't it?" Saying those words felt like spitting out razor blades.

"Oh god." Mother held me tightly. "I don't know what to believe anymore." She needed me more than ever and I was prepared to hear the truth. We attempted to put the living room back to normality, and I poured us both a neat whiskey. I know I shouldn't have indulged her, but I needed one and I doubt I could stop her, not today.

"Talk to me." This time I held her hand. She took a swig of her drink and a look of relief passed over her face as she swallowed.

Her eyes lifted from the floor and held my gaze. "I don't know if your dad hurt Sophia, but... but I know he was up to no good with her."

I was expecting it, but I couldn't stop the gasp hearing my mother admit it. "What?"

"I knew something wasn't right months before she disappeared. He kept going out at strange times, secretive conversations and coming home late. One night I followed him prepared to confront the slag, only I never expected to watch my husband pick up my daughters' best friend." Her voice shuddered with each word.

"No, they wouldn't. Dad wouldn't do that!" I still could not accept they'd do this. I felt my world fall apart again.

"I felt the same, didn't want to believe it. I saw her get into his car and she hugged him tightly." She wiped tears away. "I'm sorry I didn't support you enough when she went missing. I hated her, and I'll admit for selfish reasons I hoped she never came back" She blew her nose and put her head in her hands. "I wanted my husband back, my best friend. It was too much when I followed him again, this time he took her to the doctors. I sat in the carpark and waited for them to come out." She took in a deep breath. "She came out holding a pregnancy pack. I was devastated. The look on his face told me everything, he was terrified."

She explained how she struggled to confront him, scared to have him confirm. That was how the drinking started, it became the only way she coped.

"It was two days before she went missing that I finally found the courage to ask him. He denied it, of course. Said I was paranoid and the usual excuses." The weight seemed to fall from her shoulders, keeping this to herself must have been exhausting.

"Do you think he did do something to her?"

She tensed up but after a few seconds her shoulders dropped. "That night he went out. Popping over to the office to sort something. I knew it was a load of bollocks, but I was so drunk by that point I didn't care anymore."

"Oh Mum, I'm so sorry you've had to deal with this for so long with no support." Anger ripped through me and my sympathy for Dad disappeared. He had caused her drinking problem. I had been fooled by his pathetic act too. I was heartbroken, angry and devastated. The man I thought of as my hero had shattered our family. He was disgusting and shame washed over me. Had he got my best friend pregnant and then killed her to cover it up? Emotions ran wild around my body and the vile thoughts caused me to throw-up.

"It's OK, darling, I need to start telling the truth. As much as I know, it'll destroy us. I hate what Sophia did, but she didn't deserve to die. Her parents need closure." Tears ran like a river down her face. "I blamed her, but he was the adult, he shouldn't have done it. He knew better and the thought of him liking young girls makes me sick. It was easier to hate her, but I don't."

Suddenly above us we heard laughter, a malicious short burst. Footsteps stomped loudly along with more crashing sounds. When we made it to the landing, it was destroyed. In the middle of the rubble, a soaked Sophia stood, hands stretched out with a look of anguish on her face.

"No!" she screamed before exploding into fragments. It was silent, but we both knew what we needed to do.

Another neat whiskey before making the call. I picked up my phone and I typed out the truth or at least what we suspected, to all my friends. My finger hovered over the send button, because once I sent this, there was no going back.

"I wanted to tell you all first before I make the call. I understand if none of you ever speak to me again. Believe me when I say I am just as shocked and sickened by this. I'm sorry for what he did, so sorry." I hit send, my stomach flipped as I saw the ticks on my WhatsApp go from one, then two, then message sent

17

Making that call to the police was one of the hardest things I had ever had to do. I had essentially sent my own dad to prison. As the sun rose, I watched taking in the silence. I knew it wouldn't be long before everyone knew. I wasn't sure if my own friends were still speaking to me. Chloe had been the only one to respond. The silence from the others spoke loudly. She would stand by me; she'd promised.

I scanned the garden looking for the black and white cat that often visited, a young male cat. Cheeky and very vocal. He'd roll on the grass and bask in the sunshine for a while before heading off, back home I assumed. He didn't let me down. I heard the rattle of the gate as he jumped gracefully over, rolled and settled in his usual place. This small bit of normality calmed me. Lovely cat, thanks I thought to myself. Suddenly his ears went back, he was on his feet, back arched and his fur was puffed out.

I followed his glare. Sophia crawled from behind the green wooden shed. She was crouched like the cat in stalking mode. I thought she was going to hurt the cat. She pounced, landing on all fours but the cat was quick to make his escape. Sophia shot across the grass and disappeared along the side of the house. My back door was open. I heard the door push open all the way and the sound of deep uneven breathing got closer. The dragging sound was the worst part...rotten nails against the wooden laminated floor.

    "Kim."

    "Kim." The disembodied voice seemed to seep from every wall. *"Kimmm..."*

    I didn't have time to react before she flew through the door taking the wind out of me by knocking me to the floor. I was pinned underneath her. She snarled like a dog and water poured from her mouth and soaked me. The smell was acrid and stale...old stagnant water and rotten flesh. It was the most revolting small ever to attack my nostrils. I gagged but held back from being sick. Fighting back was a useless effort. Sophia was as strong as several men and I was trapped. Her hands gripped the sides of my head and smashed it against the floor.

Darkness descended, was I dead?

18

It's been so lonely.

I've spent so long screaming in silence, begging to be heard. She sees me now and hears my every word. The years it has taken to gain the power and strength for that to happen have seemed like a hundred years, not ten. I walked that house unable to leave until I grew stronger. My anger burned into a power and I never wanted to be this angry entity, but here I am. Using any means necessary to be heard. I am terrorizing my best friend in order to end this cycle.

I never meant to hurt Justin. I am so very sorry for what happened. I just wanted him to know too. I bet she hates me, the one thing I didn't want.

Nobody is listening, not even now. It's all so wrong how things have happened. Just like that night, I never wanted this, or to have this baby. I'm sick of never being heard.

It took so long to even understand what had happened. I thought I was being held against my will, unable to escape. I prayed someone would rescue me…dreamed of it…only there was no savior coming for me. I wouldn't see my family again, not alive anyway.

Months of walking that house drove me insane; fear and loneliness engulfed me. Then I finally saw the truth…me in that bathtub. My decaying face looking back at me. I was dead.

I remembered that night clearly after that. I didn't pass out. I remember that smash to the head and the hands 'round my throat. The rage in their eyes as they watched the life drain out of me.

I felt his presence next to me.

"Stop punishing yourself. I forgave you, it's OK."

Justin hadn't fully gained his power to haunt, as it's described. Yes, he's here. I made sure he was OK. We watched poor Kim cry by his side.

"I just want her to know I'm so sorry, for everything."

He was faint. He would pass over soon. He had no rage, just love for his wife. Once he knew she was safe and finally at peace, he would go. I hoped to go with him.

I longed to rest, to be free and happy wherever I end up. Anywhere is better than here.

"It's time to force the truth out," *I hissed. Justin nodded and gestured for me to go.*

"Help her finally see. I hate seeing her suffer and I wish I had supported her better. She will understand once this is all over. Even if the truth breaks her heart."

I left via the wall because I could. I decided who saw me, a skill I had learnt. I could still bask in the sunshine, but I didn't feel the heat. I was just a shadow, but when I needed to, I could become a hurricane. The lies some have told and the utter betrayal of some had left me full of pure disgust. Especially, one who I had thought better of...that pains me.

I know I am not innocent. I cheated on Lewis, and I never forgave myself for that. The chance of telling him how sorry I am was ripped away. The worst thing is he hates me, my Lewis. It was such a stupid idiotic mistake. I looked down at my stomach and wondered what my child would have been like and wish I had thought more about that before my death. I was scared and I just wanted it to all go away.

'He' was so angry that I didn't want to be with him, but I wanted to stay with Lewis. I remember the devastation on his face. I really had messed everything up. I knew I should have walked away and stopped it before it went too far. He'd been so nice, helped me so much and that day the stupid argument between Lewis and me had made me react...wrongly.

I passed through a group of teenagers, unseen, but one shivered. It made me smile. The little things amused me. I could be evil and mess with them, but I had other things to focus on. If my rage was at its peak I might have done more to ease my loneliness. The laughs made me miss my life, my friends and everything that came with being a kid.

The house was still the same as it had always been. They were in the kitchen washing up dishes. I waited for them to look up through the window and it didn't take long. The terror on their face made them jump backwards. The smash of the plate as it hit the floor splintering around their feet was satisfying. Eyes wide they stared. Blinking several times in hopes I would vanish. I didn't at first because the satisfaction of seeing them squirm was just enjoyable. Being murdered makes you somewhat, bitter.

For the next few days, I followed them. Everywhere they turned I was waiting. They would crack eventually.

If I could just tell Kim the truth, I would, but it doesn't work like that. Every movement I make, every time I speak is like draining a battery, so I need to draw from the energy around me. It's like moving through mud, or swimming against the tide. One movement drains me quickly, I recharge and try again. I can only muster bits of information at a time, it's frustrating.

I watched the cat in Kim's Garden. I didn't mean to scare him. I forgot that animals see me all the time. Kim was staring through the window and energy rushed through me. I shot into the house. The rage powered me forward, thinking about what was happening.

I just hope the message got through. The hands on her head was me trying to get her to see enough to know. To get justice for me and for herself and to stop the pain we have both suffered.

19

I was stunned to find my mother on my doorstep, suitcase in hand. Tears ran down her cheeks, a pathetic look on her face. The smell of wine and cigarettes on her breath.

"I need to be out of that house. I can't stand being there." Stunned, I stepped aside as the suitcase was pushed inside with her foot. "Please?"

I didn't want to have her stay with me. My home was my safe place where I could get away, but she was my mum and there was no way I could say no. We both had things to deal with. We both had been betrayed. I sighed and let her in.

"Come on in. I guess we both need the company," I said. A smile beamed over her face with the relief at not being rejected.

"Just for a few days...maybe a week."

I had enough food in my cupboard for a decent meal, sausages, and mash. I went to the kitchen and began peeling potatoes.

"What do we do now?" I asked.

"I don't know. Everyone will know soon. I don't think I can stay 'round here. I might sell up and start somewhere new, a fresh start."

I understood that because the thought had crossed my mind too. Being known as the wife and daughter of a killer was something we weren't prepared to handle.

"He's a fucking bastard," my mum snapped, banging her hand on the kitchen counter. "He ruined everything! We had a good life. Why did he have to sleep with that little tart?" Venom dripped from every word.

"Mum don't upset yourself, and don't call her that. We don't know what happened. Maybe it wasn't her fault. The way I see it, she was the child."

My mum glared at me, the disdain on her face threw me.

"What?" she snapped back. She was drunk and I could see that now. Cleverly masked as she arrived, but now her mask had slipped. She reached into her pocket and pulled out a hip flask; the smell of whiskey seeped from it. Taking a swig, she headed out the back door to smoke.

"Trust you to stick up for her."

I followed her into the garden, hoping to talk civil with her.

"I'm not! I'm confused and I love them both. It's hard to accept what I know. I am angry but I don't understand this..." She didn't reply, just swayed unsteadily on her feet.

"This is his fault, my drinking and ..." she didn't finish her sentence.

"And what?"

"What?" Mum asked, but wouldn't look at me.

"His fault for your drinking and..." I prodded, wanting to know what she was about to say.

"Nothing...just the complete fuckery he made of our marriage."

She wasn't convincing and I knew she wasn't being truthful. Why was looking me in the eye so difficult for her? I felt the cold touch on my arm and I flinched. I looked, but nothing was there. Footsteps echoed around the kitchen like bare feet on the cold tiles. My mum turned and screamed.

"No!" Terror took control of her and she backed away. "No! You stay away! Stop stalking me! You've caused enough trouble!"

Sophia appeared. Like a cat she stalked my mother. *"You lied!"* Sophia hissed, "You *betrayed him.*"

My mouth dropped open. Why was Sophia angry with my Mother?

"Tell her."

My mother was shaking her head and tried to crawl into the house. "Kim, run!"

I stood my ground. "No. We stay." I grabbed her and shook her in frustration. "She is trying to tell us something, and people need to start telling the truth! What is going on?!"

20

Sophia wouldn't leave and her gaze followed us constantly. Her eyes never leaving my mother and I knew there was more to this story. Was my dad innocent? Had my Mum thrown him to the wolves as punishment for his affair? It was likely, and the real killer wouldn't be punished.

It grew dark and every window and mirror in the house had Sophia in them. It was like being stared down by a pride of lions. It was driving us both mad.

"Make her go away!" Mother screamed. "I can't stand her face. Leave me alone!"

The radio switched on by itself and static crackled loudly. Then a voice. *"Liar, tell the truth."* Sophia's reflection in the window held her gaze on the radio. She was using the radio to communicate. *"Kim, you know it's not right. I need to be at peace."*

"I'm sorry for what he did...I'm sorry," I sobbed. She was shaking her head and the radio crackled again.

"You have nothing to be sorry for,"

there was a smile on her face. The warm one I remember as a kid.

"I miss you Kim." She was faint, losing energy and I watched as she faded away.

"I miss you too," I whispered.

My phone broke the silence and the name on the screen shocked me. I answered, not knowing what to expect.

"Lewis?"

"Kim, I've just seen your message. I've not been looking at messages. I've been in a bad place." I hear a sharp intake of breath. "I'm sorry for not being at Jay's funeral."

"I thought you hated me and I wouldn't blame you."

Silence.

"Lewis?"

"Did your dad get her pregnant?" His voice was strained. "Did he kill her?"

"Honestly, I don't know. I'm just as confused as you."

I heard the clicking of a lighter.

"Are you Ok?" he asked.

"No, I'm not."

"Can I come over? We can talk."

I wanted nothing more than to have

him around. We both had questions. "I would love to see you."

He hung up promising to be there in an hour. All I had to do was wait. I was nervous as I had to face someone outside of my family bubble. I felt a wave of shame and didn't know how things would be after this.

"Mum?" I tapped on the door, she had to stay out of it when Lewis arrived. She didn't answer. "Lewis is on his way." That made her unlock the door. Sheer horror on her face.

"What? Why?" She snapped, "He can't!"

"He's my friend and has a right to know. He's part of this too."

She slammed the door. As I walked away, I heard her scream in frustration. There was a smash, and I ignored it. Sophia watched from the hallway. "Lewis is coming. If you want to show yourself, let me know so I can prepare him." She nodded and faded away.

When Lewis arrived, he stood on the doorstep. The tension between us was alien. I hated having that distance between us. I opened my arms. He hesitated before wrapping me in the tightest hug.

"I'm sorry for being a shit friend."

"It's Ok."

We both cried at my front door, unable to move. When we eventually did, we headed inside. He settled on the sofa and I noticed his usual broad frame looked thinner. He had bags under his eyes and his usual well- groomed blonde hair looked messy and dirty.

I made us both a strong cup of tea. "Thanks." Lewis said as I passed him his mug. "Have you heard from your dad?"

I shook my head as I settled next to him. "This is such a mess."

"It's not your fault." Lewis assured me. Hearing that lifted a little bit of weight from my shoulders. We talked honestly for over an hour, and that easy feeling I thought I'd lost from our friendship quickly returned. Then while we reminisced over childhood memories, Sophia appeared behind him. Her hand outstretched towards him.

"You OK?" Lewis asked looking behind

him, following my gaze.

"I have something you need to know, but it will not be easy to take in."

He looked intrigued but a little nervous. "Can't be as bad as the past few weeks. I've been hit with all kinds of shit news." He laughed trying to lighten the mood.

"She wants to say sorry." I blurted out.

"Who?"

"Sophia."

Lewis glared at me, confusion and anger on his face. "Are you serious?" he snapped. "Jesus Kim, that's really not funny."

"I'm not laughing," I replied. My expression stayed serious. Lewis jerked up from the sofa and headed for the front door. He thought I was making this up.

"That's sick," he yelled back at me as he opened the door. He didn't make it through the door. In that moment, it was ripped from his hand and slammed shut. He stood frozen his hand outstretched.

"How did that happen?" his voice was shaky. He opened it again, but the same thing happened.

"Stop it," he begged. "It is so not funny'." Once he looked my way, he jumped stumbling backwards. His dead childhood sweetheart stood before him.

21

Lewis couldn't take his eyes off Sophia. He was speechless. Disbelief and shock had frozen him. Slowly he looked 'round at me. Sophia flickered like a flame in the wind. Lewis backed away, shaking his head. She held her hand out as if trying to pull him back. I hoped Lewis would be happy to see her, but I was wrong. He was utterly terrified, his feet tangled as he tried to get away.

"I'm not seeing her...she's not real." He was talking more to himself. Sophia looked crushed if a ghost can be. "Oh God," he put his hands over his face to block out the vision.

"Kim, this is a fucking joke, right?"

"No, Lewis. She's really here."

He slowly removed his hands clearly hoping she'd be gone. He surprised me when he spoke.

"I miss you so much, or I did." My heart sank. "Why? Why did you sleep with him...Kim's dad?"

Just at that point, a loud knocking on my door interrupted us. Sophia faded away a haunting look of sadness on her face.

"Kim!" my dad shouted through the door. My nerves were on edge. What was he doing here? Lewis flew to open the door. I wasn't quick enough to intervene. Lewis wasn't who my dad expected to greet him at the door, nor was he expecting the punch to the face.

"You sick bastard! Why did you do it?" Tears soaked Lewis's face. "She didn't deserve to die! I'll fucking kill you."

My dad was taken fully by surprise, and he fell backwards onto the front lawn. Lewis leaping at him like a mad man. Clearly his loyalty to Sophia was still strong despite her bad choices.

"She was a child."

"I didn't do anything!" my dad cried, pleading to be heard. "Please, you need to listen! I didn't..." the crunching blow cut off my dad's words. The daughter in me rushed to the surface.

"Stop, Lewis, Stop." I dragged him off and Lewis scuttled backwards, the red mist fading.

"Please, Kim. Listen to me." Dad's

eyes were wide with fear and desperation. "I can explain everything." His hands clasped together like he was in prayer.

"It's time I was honest. I should have been honest at the start. I knew what it would look like and didn't want to cause us, as a family, any trouble. I was an idiot because it happened anyway." There was an honesty in his voice.

"Inside." I said firmly. The neighbors would be having a field day. I helped my dad up from my crushed flowerbed while blood dripped down his chin from the broken nose.

"You aren't seriously letting him inside?" Lewis asked, disbelief in his voice. He was still shaking, his fists clenched. I threw Lewis a warning glare.

"He is still my Dad, and I want to hear what he has to say." Holding a handful of tissues to his nose dad settled at the kitchen table. I heard the footsteps running down the stairs. They had purpose. My mum flew into the kitchen full of utter disgust. "What is HE doing here?"

"If people would let me talk. I will tell

you."

"Why are you not behind bars you sick murdering ..." Dad's hand was outstretched, hushing my mum. "Stop! Enough is enough."

I made coffee and handed a mug to everyone...extra strong for the drunk in the room. She could listen instead of hiding in a bottle of booze. I took a cigarette from my mother's packet. It was one of those times.

"Dad, I'm listening."

22

My dad looked up from the floor, hands clasped together.

"I never slept with Sophia, I'm not a pedophile. I was trying to help her." Mum snorted and began shaking her hand. "Liar!"

"The police have taken my DNA. I am not the father of the baby, and I know the test will prove it. Sophia was upset one day. She was walking through Havant, and I had stopped at the bank. I took her for a coffee at Costa. At first, she wouldn't tell me what was wrong. Then after some reassurance, she finally broke down in tears and she admitted she was pregnant. I assumed as anyone would that it was your baby." My dad pointed at Lewis. "She was so scared and confused."

"Who was she sleeping with?" Lewis asked, "I want to know."

"Yeah, I know. But it will shock you."

Lewis shrugged, "I don't care."

"Sophia needed support. I gave her that. I made sure she saw a doctor and helped her to decide. Sophia wanted to put the child up for adoption. She wasn't ready to bring up a child but couldn't bring herself to have an abortion. It was the most sensible solution."

His story sounded genuine. Was my dad caught up in this because he had just been trying to help a scared sixteen-year-old? I held on to some hope that he wasn't some sick child killer.

"Thank you." A faint hand appeared on my dads' shoulder and the radio crackled. Sophia stood flickering. The shocked reactions from both Lewis and my dad sent her away. She hadn't wanted to scare them.

"Fucking hell," Dad said, breathless. His hand against his chest. "Kim, what..." I interrupted my father before he could finish.

"I've been seeing Sophia for a while and have been trying to help her get justice." I reassured him she wouldn't hurt them. My dad was telling the truth, I knew that now. Sophia had clarified that.

"Dad, I'm so sorry." I threw my arms round him. "How could I think such a thing?"

His strong arms held me tightly. "It's OK, baby. I should have been honest ten years ago. When she went missing, I panicked. I knew what people would think."

Relief washed over me. I hadn't lost my hero. He had been the man I knew he was. A caring man just trying to help a vulnerable girl. My best friend.

"NO!" my mum screamed. "No!" She was hysterical. "He's lying! I saw you together at your secret meetings!"

He looked at his wife with pity on his face. "You never let me explain. You drank and belittled me. I thought the stress of it all had caused it. I tried to help you."

I watched as my mum collapsed to the floor. "I don't believe you. You, you ..." her hands flew to her face. "Oh God, what have I done?"' Sophia was back flickering behind my mother.

"They all deserve the truth now, Kim." Sophia said her hand reaching for me. *"Give me your hand."*

I held my hand out and she placed hers on mine. It felt cool, like putting my hand in cold water. I collapsed to the floor as Sophia took control of my mind.

I looked at myself in a mirror and Sophia looked back me. All my own memories sucked from my mind.

23

DECEMBER 5TH, 2009

Sophia pushed down her worries.

Nobody could tell I was pregnant. I was still in the first trimester. Soon I wouldn't be able to hide it though. The small bump was still easy to conceal. I would get through today and sit my parents down and tell them, and what I have decided. I was sixteen and I couldn't have a baby, but I wasn't sure I could have an abortion either. I was more scared than I had ever been. The pregnancy itself was bad enough, but once people knew they would also know I had betrayed Lewis.

Kim would be so upset about me keeping things from her, but I feel so ashamed. I rested my hand on my tummy and made a promise that I would do whatever was right for us both.

The wave of nausea hit me, every day at the same time and I had to lie down. Morning sickness wasn't fun. Although it was more mid-afternoon, I felt like utter crap for an hour. I waited for it to subside and fixed my hair and make-up. I could hear my Mum chatting excitedly on the phone, ensuring everything was ready for my party. I think she was more excited about it than me. I smiled at her happiness knowing that would change after I told her my secret. She'd be devastated. Pregnant at sixteen wasn't what you wanted for your daughter. My dad would hunt the father down and...oh God what a mess. I was a stupid idiot. The two times Lewis and I had sex; we'd been so careful. But one ridiculous moment and I had ruined everything. It was all my fault. Fear gripped me at that point, and I didn't want everyone to know. Only one person knew and that would be how it stayed.

Kim called bringing me out of my trance and I forced a smile when I answered. I sounded happy just the way she'd expect me to. Pretending to be OK was exhausting, but she always made me feel like we could take on the world. That's why she was my best friend.

During the party, I chatted with family and friends. I smiled, I danced, and I was enjoying myself. Maybe things would be

OK. Then a text came through on my phone, a number I didn't recognize. I went to the ladies and locked myself in a cubicle. I stared at my phone and felt the walls closing in on me.

"I know what you have done."

It was obvious what they were referring to and another message came through naming a time and place to meet before they exposed my secret.

I needed to get away without anyone seeing me leave. Kim came in as I was about to leave the ladies and I was dragged onto the dancefloor. I let several songs play out before making my excuse and as the party noise faded into the background, I looked back. The thought of that being the last time I would ever see my family and friends again, never entered my head.

I walked down into Havant, irritated I had left without my jacket because I was frozen. The adrenaline kept me moving. It was the darkness of the Billy line at that time of night that made me consider going back to the party, until another text came through.

"Hurry up before I post your secret online."

The nausea hit me again, but it wasn't due to the baby. It was because of dread and panic.

I was walking into a situation I wasn't prepared for, but if they could out me before I was ready, I had to stop it. Each step sounded louder along with the crunching underneath my feet. The darkness was closing in like a black fog. I was terrified, but my secret being exposed terrified me more.

The abandoned house stood in front of me...like a scene from a movie. I swallowed down the fear and found the secret way in. It was silent inside and there was no sign of anyone else. Ok, I'll wait another five minutes and then I'll leave. Someone was pranking me, I decided, and laughed at myself for being so stupid. This was so Matt and Justin's sense of humor. Those daft idiots. I would return to the party and they would be rolling around in stitches. The relief was short lived, as I was about to leave footsteps behind me froze me on the spot.

"Who is there?" *I asked, my voice low and shaky. I wasn't alone. In the darkness, someone approached and I slowly turned around. I could see their outline, but it was too dark to see their face.*

"Look at you, all sweet and innocent." *The voice was hard as stone.* "If only they all knew what a little slut you really are."

I could smell whiskey and the voice had a slur to it. They stumbled as they walked forward. A shiver went down my spine as I processed the voice. I knew it well.

"Look, I don't know what you think you know..."

"Shut the fuck up!" *they snapped,* "Don't play me for a fucking fool. I know you have been shagging my husband."

Her words hit me like a tornado. "What?" *The fury in her eyes as she lurched towards me. It was Kathy Jennings. Kim's Mum thought I was sleeping with her husband. How could she think that? I was so confused, but she wasn't waiting for me to explain. I raced down the hall, but she was quicker than me. Grabbing my arm, she spun me 'round.*

"I hope it was worth it. Destroying your best friend's family." *Spit soaked my face.* "You think you are going to steal my husband from me!?"

"Kathy, please calm down, I haven't ..." *she punched me so hard, I fell to the floor.* "You have got this wrong, I haven't slept with Dennis! Oh my God, no way! He's like so old. Gross!"

Nothing got through to her. The more I spoke, the more it angered her. She continued to attack throwing punches to my head. I crawled away. My only escape access was the stairs. I used every bit of energy to climb them.

Kathy gained on me quickly. She grabbed my hair and threw me into the bathroom.

"Kathy, please." *I scrambled backwards begging for her to let me explain,* "Dennis hasn't done anything!"

"Don't lie! I've seen you meeting in secret. His hushed calls and it makes me sick. You were like family to me!" *her voice climbing higher the more hysterical she became. Kathy had this crazed look on her*

*face, and this was when I suddenly feared
for my life.*

"It was bad enough knowing what you
were up to behind my back, but you go
and get yourself pregnant."

"It isn't Dennis's baby! You have to
believe me." *I begged, pushing myself up
from the floor.* "I made a stupid mistake,
but it's not what you think."

"You'll say anything," *she snarled in
my face.*

"Look what you made me do.
Little Bitch ..."

"I cheated on Lewis...yes, but it wasn't
with you husband. He's too old, seriously!
It's Adam's baby."

*She hit me again and I fell backwards.
The pain ripped through my body as my
head hit the rusty taps and blood poured
from my head. I was wet. The bath was
full of old stagnant water. I screamed so
loud if anyone were nearby, I know I would
be heard.*

"You crazy bitch. I'll get you sent to
prison for this!" *Kathy had a look of horror
on her face, a realization that she'd gone
too far.* "It's all you fault. You should have

kept your knickers on."

Then, as I begged for my life, her hands closed around my neck, and I was forced under the water. I tried to fight back, I fought for my life until all I saw was darkness.

The tiles on my kitchen floor came back into focus along with the sobs of my mother as she begged for me to talk to her.

"What did she do to you? Kim?"

I couldn't look at her. My mum had killed Sophia. I took some deep breaths forcing the vomit back down.

"Kim?" My dad knelt beside me. "Are you OK?" I grabbed for his hand. "Call the police."

"What? Why?"

"Because I know who killed Sophia."

I looked at my mother sprawled on the kitchen floor, a sobbing mess. "She showed me what happened. Time to tell the truth."

The wail that escaped from my mum tore at my every nerve. "I'm so sorry. I didn't mean it." She collapsed at that point. "I didn't mean to kill her. Please forgive me. I thought..."

My dad looked at his wife, the women he had been with and thought he knew for the past twenty-nine years, with horror, heartbreak, and pain.

"You...killed Sophia? Kathy...?"

"Dennis please forgive me."

"You thought I had slept with a schoolgirl and killed her for it. How can I ever forgive that?" The disgust in his voice tore away any hope from my Mum. I couldn't back her on this because I felt the same. Disgust and shame.

Lewis's eyes bored into my mother and my dad held him back from attacking her.

"I know son, I know, but let the police deal with her. I'm sorry. I really am. I had no idea." Lewis collapsed into his arms and sobbed.

Violence wouldn't solve this, and it was time for her to face her punishment.

I walked to the kitchen table, picked up my phone and made the hardest call I ever had to make.

24

I packed up my last box, labelled it, and handed it to my dad. I took one last look at the home I once shared with Justin. After the truth came out about my mother, I could no longer stay. The abuse and the whispers on the street became too much.

Six months had passed, and my mother was four weeks into a life sentence. I tried to understand her reasons why, but I couldn't forgive her. Nothing could excuse her actions. I had visited once to see if I couldn't find a way to get past it, but the answer was no. She had murdered Sophia, left her to rot alone, and was happy to let my dad take the blame.

"That's it. Time to go." The removal vans were ready to take everything into storage. We were heading to Spain. My parents had a holiday home out in Valencia and while we decided how to rebuild our lives, we would live there. My dad was broken by all this, and for his sake I wanted to save him from the British media.

"I have one last call to make." I dialed the number and waited.

"Hello?"

"Adam?"

"Hey, Kim."

"How are you holding up?" I asked, and Adam burst into tears.

"I'm trying to get through it. Lewis won't talk to me. I guess I deserve that."

The truth was that it had been Adam that Sophia had slept with. After helping her so much with her schoolwork and because of a stupid argument with Lewis, she'd turned to Adam. The DNA had match him as the father which was a shock for him to hear. This had broken all of us. Our once close friendship had been rocked to its core. Chloe had flown back to LA once Sophia had been put to rest and who knows if she will ever come back. Lewis didn't want any reminders and I would be one of the worst ones. Sophia's parents couldn't believe it, and understandably never wanted to see any of us again. Seeing their faces at Mum's sentencing won't be something I could ever erase, hatred, pure and simple. Who could blame them? My mother had killed their child over a misunderstanding. They had sent my Dad a message thanking him for trying to help, but his lies had caused her death. In their eyes, he was just as guilty and in some ways, he agreed with them. He will live with this until he takes his last breath.

Sometimes you can't mend the things that are too painful, but maybe we could move on now. Even if that means without each other.

"Adam, I don't hate you. I just wanted to make sure you were OK? Take Care."

I hung up and scanned the house once more before locking the door one last time. There was a sound at my feet and Pearl meowed from her box.

"Are you ready girl?" The cat was coming with us. She was one beautiful part of our past that remained.

As my dad pulled out of the drive and pulled away, I looked behind one last time.

Tears fell as Sophia stood with Justin. She was finally able to rest, and Justin would go with her. At least I knew they were both at peace.

"Things will be OK," dad promised. My old life faded into the background just like Sophia and Justin, but a new life could finally begin.

ABOUT THE AUTHOR

Deep in the heart of Portsmouth, England, lives a quirky Brit with a larger-than-life imagination.

Meet Kat Green!

Music and the Military have been major influences in Kat's life and has shaped the woman she is today. Kat moved around frequently growing up which afforded her the opportunity to meet new people and experience many different bands broadening her music library. Writing was always an afterthought, but when she lost her Mum to cancer in 2010, it was time to put words to paper. Life is too short.

Kat's books span the rock star romance genre adding a hint of mystery with her Black Eagles Series. Or if you need a paranormal thriller to keep you looking over your shoulder at night, check out Veiled, Frozen Pact, or her latest release, Listen To Me! Either way, you will not be disappointed.

Please feel free to follow Kat on various social media platforms so you never miss out on a new release!

Facebook: https://www.facebook.com/KatGrn00/
Amazon: https://www.amazon.com/Kat-Green/e/B00L2MQE0A
BookBub: http://bit.ly/2Wiu4g9
Twitter: https://twitter.com/Katwrites00

More works by Kat Green

Strings (The Black Eagles Series Book 1)

Encore (The Black Eagles Series Book 2)

Finale (The Black Eagles Series Book 3)

Veiled

Frozen Pact

Surviving The Game

Follow on Social Media